PENGUIN CLASSICS

A HERO OF OUR TIME

MIKHAIL YURIEVICH LERMONTOV was born in 1814. After his mother's death in 1817, he was separated from his father and brought up at the estate of his aristocratic grandmother. Educated at home, he twice made journeys to the Caucasus and then studied in Moscow University Pension for the Nobility and the University (1830–32), although without sitting examinations. He then entered St. Petersburg Guards' School and began writing poetry and autobiographical dramas in prose. In 1834 he was made an officer in the Guards Hussars. On Pushkin's death in 1837, Lermontov was arrested for a poem of invective against court circles, *The Death of a Poet,* and was consequently expelled from the Guards and sent to the army in the Caucasus. When he returned to the capital he became involved in a duel and in 1840 was banished again to the Caucasus. He was twice cited for bravery, but the tsar refused to give him the award. On leave in 1841, hoping to retire and devote himself to literature, he was ordered back to the forces. He was challenged to a duel by another officer over a trivial insult and was killed on the spot. Lermontov is renowned as the one true Romantic poet produced by Russia and the one who reflected most strongly the current trend of Byronism. Many of his poems were set to music— *Borodino* and *The Cossack Lullaby* became popular songs and *The Demon* was made into an opera by A. Rubenstein. His other poems include *The Novice, The Prayer, Novgorod, The Prophet,* and *My Country.* Lermontov greatly influenced Dostoevsky and Blok, while Tolstoy and Chekhov regarded his prose as a model.

NATASHA RANDALL has published translations of Yevgeny Zamyatin's *We* (shortlisted for the 2008 Oxford-Weidenfeld Translation Prize) and Osip Mandelstam's poetry, as well as the work of contemporary writers Arkady Dragomoshchenko, Alexander Skidan, and Olga Zondberg. She is a frequent contributor to the *Los Angeles Times* and lives in London.

NEIL LABUTE is a filmmaker and playwright whose work includes *In the Company of Men* and *The Shape of Things.* He lives in Chicago.

MIKHAIL LERMONTOV

A Hero of Our Time

Translated with an Introduction and Notes by
NATASHA RANDALL

Foreword by NEIL LABUTE

PENGUIN BOOKS

PENGUIN BOOKS

Published by the Penguin Group

Penguin Group (USA) Inc., 375 Hudson Street,
New York, New York 10014, U.S.A.
Penguin Group (Canada), 90 Eglinton Avenue East, Suite 700, Toronto,
Ontario, Canada M4P 2Y3 (a division of Pearson Penguin Canada Inc.)
Penguin Books Ltd, 80 Strand, London WC2R 0RL, England
Penguin Ireland, 25 St Stephen's Green, Dublin 2
Ireland (a division of Penguin Books Ltd)
Penguin Group (Australia), 250 Camberwell Road, Camberwell,
Victoria 3124, Australia (a division of Pearson Australia Group Pty Ltd)
Penguin Books India Pvt Ltd, 11 Community Centre,
Panchsheel Park, New Delhi – 110 017, India
Penguin Group (NZ), 67 Apollo Drive, Rosedale, North Shore 0632,
New Zealand (a division of Pearson New Zealand Ltd)
Penguin Books (South Africa) (Pty) Ltd, 24 Sturdee Avenue,
Rosebank, Johannesburg 2196, South Africa

Penguin Books Ltd, Registered Offices:
80 Strand, London WC2R 0RL, England

This translation first published in Penguin Books 2009

1 3 5 7 9 10 8 6 4 2

Translation, introduction and notes copyright © Natasha Randall, 2009
Foreword copyright © Neil LaBute, 2009
All rights reserved

LIBRARY OF CONGRESS CATALOGING IN PUBLICATION DATA
Lermontov, Mikhail Ur'evich, 1814–1841.
[Geroi nashego vremeni. English]
A hero of our time / Mikhail Lermontov ; translated with an introduction and
notes by Natasha Randall ; foreword by Neil Labute.
p. cm.—(Penguin classics)
"This translation first published in Penguin Books 2009."
Includes bibliographical references.
ISBN 978-0-14-310563-3
1. Caucasus—Fiction.   2. Russia—Social life and customs—1533–1917—Fiction.
3. Russia—History, Military—1801–1917—Fiction.   I. Title.
PG3337.L4G4133   2009
891.73'3—dc22   2009006797

Printed in the United States of America
Set in Sabon

Contents

Foreword

Mikhail Lermontov finished writing his novel, *A Hero of Our Time,* at roughly the same age that I was working in a Blockbuster video store and annually flunking a remedial math course in college. I may have those dates wrong, but it's pretty darn close. I'm one of those people who often compares their artistic progress to the work of a few of their literary heroes, and Lermontov was one of them. Georg Büchner was another, and he had written all of his works and was dead by twenty-three (he also found the time to become a medical doctor, but that's just plain annoying). Orson Welles terrified America by roughly that same age with his *War of the Worlds* radio broadcast and had also made what most critics describe as "the best film ever made" (*Citizen Kane*) by twenty-six. If I'm not mistaken, I think I passed that math class at about the same age.

Lermontov, of course, didn't live long after the publication of his first prose work (a bullet in a duel saw to that), but he effectively helped chart the course for the modern Russian novel with one stroke. Like a few others—Shakespeare being perhaps the godfather of the bunch—Lermontov began writing in a psychological manner before the term really had any weight to it and well before Freud started seeing the word *sex* floating in every cup of coffee (and still had the use of his own jaw). One could carry on at some length and gush intellectually about all of Lermontov's influences and influential works, but most of you would know that I simply looked him up on Wikipedia and that I'm really just reciting somebody else's research back to you. I'd rather try to be truthful and express a little respect toward someone who stumbled onto a way of working that, within the confines of one short prose work, actually advanced the way we see and think and feel about the novel.

The character of Grigory Alexandrovich Pechorin is one that amuses as much as he distresses. After you have finished reading Lermontov's work you are thankful it's only a novel, but you're also quite sure it's a truthful portrait of the artist as a young soldier. Much has been made of how autobiographical or not Lermontov's personality sketch of Pechorin is. In the end, though, that hardly seems to matter. Whether emerging from a poisoned look in the mirror or derived from a thousand details of his friends and neighbors, Lermontov gets the alchemy just right and creates one of the most vivid and persuasive portraits of the male ego ever put down on paper. Everyone from Dostoyevsky to Palahniuk needs to thank Lermontov for not shying away from his "warts and all" creation and for setting the literary bar so damn high. It's not for nothing that writers like both Turgenev and Chekhov have commented on the ruthless honesty with which Lermontov wrote. Indeed, Chekhov was rumored to have remarked, "Still just a boy, and he wrote that!" (I'm sure if Mr. Chekhov had been flunking a math class he would've been even more impressed.)

There are some terrific and clever uses of structure in Lermontov's work—the diary sections juxtaposed with the other two tales, the multiple narrators, etc.—but I am most taken with his precise and ruthless approach to character. Lermontov never tries to fully explain Pechorin's behavior, and, most important, he never apologizes for it. This is psychology at its most advanced. Let the critics and the scholars sit about and ponder over the "why" of it all—Lermontov dumps the facts and exploits of his character into the laps of his readers and lets them do some of the work for a change. He writes with the precision of a surgeon but with the heart of Caligula. The life of Pechorin is to be seen, episode for episode, as both a cautionary tale and a wonderful feat of derring-do. If there's a modern equivalent in popular literature, it's probably George MacDonald Fraser's hilarious Flashman series. What a treat it would be to have Pechorin and Flashman meet on the field of battle, perhaps in the Crimean (Pechorin would have to keep himself alive somehow for another decade or so, but it's possible); the Russian might've been very surprised to finally meet his match in the silly, dangerous, and probably sociopathic form of Fraser's Englishman.

All this talk of psychology and I only now get to the word *sociopath*. Is there room in the profile of Pechorin to really make a case for it? I think so, and perhaps he's even one of the very first in serious Western literature—except for maybe Aaron the Moor in *Titus Andronicus* and a few other characters who pop up in Jacobean and Restoration drama. Oh, and that one other fellow. You know the one, created by a certain Mr. de Laclos a good fifty years or so before Lermontov started writing prose. Valmont, the chilling central figure of *Les Liaisons Dangereuses,* is another example of man at his darkest and certainly had to be a beacon toward which the young writer Lermontov steered his literary vessel. How could a character as rich and complex as Valmont not spur Lermontov on in his own work, helping him to create this puzzle of a soldier, one who becomes more complex and distant the more you learn about him? That type of literary figure—one that threads through Büchner's Woyzeck to Welles's Kane to Mamet's Edmond—who time and again intrigues and frightens us with even measure. For who of us is ever really knowable, in the end? Certainly not Pechorin and probably not his creator, either. And that's just fine by me. (I just wish he hadn't been so damn young when he wrote it!)

Something that's rarely discussed in appreciations of Mikhail Lermontov is his work as a visual artist. He was a painter of some distinction, and his nature paintings of the Caucasus Mountains—a place that he knew both from his youth and from his being assigned there twice as a soldier for behavior unbecoming—are masterly in their use of color and in the persuasive sense of detail. That kind of artist's eye is always visible in *A Hero of Our Time.* I don't know the

poetic work of Lermontov well enough to comment—that's
what Google is for, kids—but I admire the hell out of him
for writing a prose work of such complexity and for such ef-
fortless command over character. Thank God he wasn't a
dramatist or I'd hate the guy even more. I think he would've
been a fine one, however; anyone who can probe so willingly
and with such a breathless sense of candor can no doubt
write a play. I think that's the thing that playwrights and
novelists need above all else today—more than a sense of
structure or some MFA from an expensive school: a love of
danger and a willingness to be a spelunker of the human
soul. Writing is not for pussies.

I know that the critical reaction was all over the map for
A Hero of Our Time, and that warms my heart. You know
you've done a good day's work when you've split the critical
community in two (or three or four). Lermontov lived only
a year or so past the publication of his novel and so didn't
have the chance to respond with any additional work. I'd
like to believe he would've spat in the face of popular opinion, though, and would've written exactly what he wanted
without caring too much about what anybody else had to
say. Anyone who creates a Pechorin doesn't appear to worry
much about what society thinks of him. Lermontov was shot
in a duel by someone he'd known for most of his life; apparently the man (a Major N. S. Martynov, to give him his lim-
ited due) was angry at Lermontov for some public jibes and
challenged him to a duel. Lermontov, like his literary creation before him, took it like a man and said yes. That's an
almost perfect way for a writer to die, really, when you think
about it. It's symbolic of the relationship we have with our
critics—we challenge them with our work, and they respond
to us through their weekly reviews—and then we die, either
onstage or off. It doesn't really matter if anyone likes us or
if we sell tickets, but it's in the fact that we continue to do it;
time and again we artists create something and put ourselves
out there in the public to be read and discussed and even
ridiculed. The fact is, it's guys like Lermontov who are the
brave ones, the ones who—despite the jokes and debauchery

and the jaundiced worldviews—keep riding off into the valley of darkness. Hell, anybody can sit up on the grassy knoll and blog about it afterward.

God bless writers. How can I not admire a bunch of brave, drunk sociopaths who keep doing the same thing that I love to do? Lermontov showed us the path. All we have to do is keep getting back up on the horse. Sounds perfectly reasonable to me.

Of course, I was still flunking a math class at the age of twenty-six, so beware.

NEIL LABUTE

Introduction

Grigory Alexandrovich Pechorin is a hero without a cause—to pervert a latter-day aphorism. He is a cynical young man who fights duels, seduces maidens, hunts wild boar, and stirs up trouble. He will tell you this himself: "I run through the memory of my past in its entirety and can't help asking myself: why have I lived? For what purpose was I born? . . . There probably was one once, and I probably did have a lofty calling, because I feel a boundless strength in my soul . . . But I didn't divine this calling. I was carried away with the bait of passions, empty and unrewarding. I came out of their crucible as hard and cold as iron, but I had lost forever the ardor for noble aspirations, the best flower of life . . ."

His questions are as relevant today as ever, but Pechorin's story takes place in the 1830s. Nicholas the First was on the throne, despised by the Russian intelligentsia for his repression of discourse. He had crushed the Decembrist revolt, which had attempted to prevent his ascendancy to the throne. In his book on Russian literature, Maurice Baring describes Nicholas the First's rule as "a regime of patriarchal supervision, government interference, rigorous censorship, and iron discipline." The decade was a time of constraints, when young men like Pechorin felt stifled and ineffectual.

Lermontov's hero is serving in the army, based in the Caucasus, where Russian forces are attempting to subdue its mountain tribes. This mountainous region to the south of Russia today encompasses lands such as Chechnya, Georgia, Armenia, North Ossetia, South Ossetia, and Dagestan.

National boundaries have changed over time, but one cannot underestimate the metaphysical place that the Caucasian landscape fills in the Russian consciousness: it is the landscape "where in the mountains martial robbery occurs and the savage genius of inspiration is hiding in the mute silence" (Pushkin, *The Prisoner of the Caucasus*). Lermontov is often called the "poet of the Caucasus" and it is no surprise, given his descriptions of the terrain: "What a glorious place . . . ! On every side there are unassailable mountains, and reddish promontories, hung with green ivy and crowned with clumps of plane trees; there are yellow precipices, covered with the lines of gullies; and right up high: a gold fringe of snow."

Picture these mountains where *dzhigits,* skilled horsemen, twirl their steeds on jagged promontories; where *abreks,* Caucasian freedom fighters, roam the hills in hordes, adhering to nothing but their own moral code; where the chimneys of *saklyas,* mountain huts, send up smoke, visible to travelers from across vast valleys. The Caucasus was home to some of the fiercest Cossacks, who fought with the Russians in their efforts to conquer the mountain regions. They were also assisted by so-called peaceable princes (tribal leaders who cooperated with Russian forces). If a soldier was fortunate, he might become a *kunak* of such a peaceable prince—a sworn friend, an adopted brother, on whom great generosity was bestowed. Both the ethnic groups and the languages of the Caucasus are many and varied. These mountains are home to Georgians, Lezghians, Ossetians, Circassians, and Chechens, among others. According to an anecdote told by Edmund Spencer in his *Travels in Circassia, Krim Tartary, Etcetera* of 1837, when a Turkish sultan sent a learned man to discover the languages of the Caucasus, he returned with just a bag of pebbles. When the sultan asked the man to present his findings, the man shook the bag of pebbles—it was the best imitation he could conjure, having failed in the hopeless task of learning anything of them. The literary critic Vissarion Belinsky remarked in 1841: "It is a strange business! It is as if the Caucasus is destined to be the cradle of our poetic talents, to be the inspirer and bear-cub of their muse, the poetic motherland!"[1]

While its setting may be very exotic and remote, the historical position of *A Hero of Our Time* places it right in the thick of things literary. It is a pivotal book that sits on the cusp between Romanticism and Realism, at a moment when Russian literature was forging its path from poetry to the novel. Until 1840, Russian writers had merely flirted with the novel. As the Russian literary critic Boris Eikhenbaum wrote, "Lermontov died early, but this fact bears no relation to the historical work which he accomplished, and changes nothing in the resolution of the literary-historical problem which interests us. It was necessary to sum up the classical period of Russian poetry and to prepare the transition to the creation of a new prose. History demanded it—and it was accomplished by Lermontov."[2] Pushkin had just died after producing short stories and his famous novel-in-verse, *Eugene Onegin,* and Dostoevsky, Turgenev, and Tolstoy had yet to emerge. Gogol was writing prose but had produced only short stories until this point. With his book, the young Lermontov, only twenty-six when he wrote *A Hero of Our Time,* called the Russian novel into being.

As a writer, Lermontov is said to have been influenced by the works of Byron, Chateaubriand, Constant, and, of course, Pushkin. The novel with which *A Hero of Our Time* is often compared is Alfred de Musset's *La Confession d'un Enfant du Siècle* for their similar titles and descriptions of moral malaise. In turn, Chekhov, Dostoevsky, and Tolstoy were each influenced by Lermontov—his metaphysics, his ironic stances, and his descriptions of the Caucasus. But, as scholar John Garrard explains in his essay "Old Wine in New Bottles: The Legacy of Lermontov," *A Hero of Our Time* occupies a special place in the development of Russian literature:

> [F]ar too much time is spent tracking down possible domestic and foreign sources for his works and far too little time is given over to an exploration of what Eikhenbaum called many

years ago Lermontov's "art of fusion" (*iskusstvo splava*), his ability to combine a variety of available elements into a new and original form. . . . It is arguably true that Lermontov had a more lasting impact on the shape and contours of the Russian novel than either Pushkin or Gogol. *A Hero of Our Time* possesses three of the most central characteristics of the Russian novel: 1) psychological analysis; 2) concern with ideas; 3) sociopolitical and ethical awareness. None of these features is the exclusive property of the novel in Russia, but the intensity with which they are engaged does help define the Russian novel and differentiate it from the novel elsewhere.[3]

As a piece of social commentary, *A Hero of Our Time* created quite a stir when it emerged, immediately garnering both praise and criticism. It came out at a time when the debate between Slavophiles and Westerners about Russian cultural identity was coming to a crescendo. Slavophile critics such as S. P. Shevyrev and Apollon Grigoriev complained that Pechorin represented the vices of the West, not of Russia. Belinsky, on the other hand, defended the work's validity as a portrait of a Russian type by placing it as descendant from Pushkin's *Eugene Onegin*.

Indeed, as Vladimir Nabokov describes in a piece called "The Lermontov Mirage" (*The Russian Review*, November 1941), Pechorin and Onegin may be cut from the same cloth—but fashions have changed in Lermontov's hands:

> In Russian schools, at least in my day, a favorite theme for compositions was "Onegin and Pechorin." The parallel is obvious, but quite superficial. Pushkin's Onegin stretches himself throughout the book and yawns. Lermontov's Pechorin does nothing of the sort—he laughs and bites. With his immense store of tenderness, kindness, and heroism behind his cynical and arrogant appearance, he is a deeper personality than the cold lean fop so delightfully depicted by Pushkin.

Indeed, *A Hero of Our Time* is a much greater step toward the Russian novel as we know it largely because it is an effort in prose, which adjusts narrative perspectives from poetical practices. In broad terms, traditional prose lends more dimension to a character than traditional poetry. John Stuart Mill wrote that "all poetry is of the nature of soliloquy," that when we read poetry we are somehow overhearing the poet, who is addressing himself. Epic poems and novels in verse belong more to the category of sung stories, where the narration is delivered from the poet or bard to his audience. Novels, on the other hand, expand the notions of narration by exploring perspectives. The poem requires you to suspend disbelief—you must agree to its terms. A novel is an act of persuasion of the reader—it seduces a reader into believing it. As the Russian literary canon goes, you could say Onegin is the ready, Pechorin is the aim, and the rest are the fire.

Much has been made of the narrative structure of this novel—which has three narrators in total. The story emerges over the course of various episodes that aren't chronologically ordered. In fact, originally the novel wasn't written as one singular work. Lermontov published most of these various episodes separately in journals such as "Notes of the Fatherland" in 1839 and early 1840. He put it all together for publication in 1841. As he did so, one can only assume that he had the liberty to rearrange the text as he saw fit, to sew it into a chronological narrative. But Lermontov chose to leave it in its prismatic, nonlinear, patchwork form. It is a portrait of a man, not a simple tale per se. Most nineteenth-century novelists in the European and later the Russian tradition gave us their characters chronologically intact, showing us their development over the course of time. This is not the case in *A Hero of Our Time*. If they were delivered in sequential order, the stories would read, "Taman," "Princess Mary," "Bela," "The Fatalist," "Maxim Maximych," and, finally, the Foreword to Pechorin's diary. In fact, if you're looking for the ending, it appears as a mere comment on page 55, at the beginning of the Foreword to Pechorin's Journal. But that's irrelevant—you can't ruin the ending of this book. The book is a portrait, told as a page-turning adventure story, a psychological look at a young man who exemplified the frustrating quandary of his type. Pechorin is a literary prototype of the "superfluous man" of Russian literature; he is another version of the Byronic antihero; and he is an early model of what would later become a nihilist.

A Hero of Our Time gives us Pechorin delivered from a few different angles, but there is nothing static about this depiction. The hero himself doesn't evolve exactly, but during the progress of the novel Lermontov brings the reader ever closer to its hero. The first narrator listens to Maxim Maximych, a staff captain posted alongside Pechorin, who describes at length his experiences with our hero. Then this narrator, together with Maxim Maximych, encounters Pechorin himself. And finally, we are given Pechorin's journal—an episode in a dark corner of Russia near the Sea of Azov and an episode that occurs in a pocket of high society in the Russian spa town of Pyatigorsk—all from the horse's mouth. Lermontov doesn't sacrifice any suspense with this structure but rather gives us his hero in ever-closer increments and builds delightful anticipation in so doing.

As C. J. G. Turner writes, "The absence of the author, in the sense of a guiding point of view, is a fundamental—and distinctly modern—feature of *A Hero of Our Time*. Instead, the values of the text are nicely balanced, leaving the reader free to be primarily repelled by the immorality of Pechorin, or fascinated by his personality . . ." There are two inroads for the reader into Pechorin's character—the first is this narrative movement, which becomes increasingly intimate, culminating in Pechorin's diary. The second is through the perceptions of the characters surrounding Pechorin. Each begins with admiration for him and eventually feels betrayed. Maxim Maximych describes him as "a wonderful fellow, I dare say," only to feel snubbed by him afterward. Grushnitsky is his friend, and later his adversary. Princess Mary falls in love with him, and sheds many tears as time goes on. Meanwhile, his journals show a sense of poetry, evidence of higher education, and a love of nature. He is self-reflective and sometimes contrite. In a review in 1840, Belinsky wrote that, "In his very vices, a certain greatness shines through, like lightning through black storm-clouds, and he is beautiful and full of poetry, even at those moments when our human feeling is roused against him . . ."[4] A simple reading has the reader looking for redemption in Pechorin but experiencing a cycle of hopes and disappointments along the way. Some adore his roguishness and derring-do. Others find him repellent and exhausting.

In the preface to Pechorin's diaries, which is written by the book's first narrator, a nameless travel writer, we are given the contradiction of the work: "Perhaps several readers will want to know my opinion of Pechorin's character? My reply is the title of this book. 'What vicious irony!' they will say. I don't know." A lot has been written about the ironic content of *A Hero of Our Time*. Pechorin's remarks are often ironic and indeed sarcastic. The title might be both of these. The reader is constantly invited to reject a literal interpretation of the text. But the beauty of this fiction, and all fiction, is that literal and ironic readings can coexist. Things seem to be one thing and turn out to be another—a novel is a long and nuanced answer to a question. As Roland Barthes wrote, "the essence of writing is to prevent any reply to the question—who is speaking?"[5] And in the author's preface, which was added to the second edition of the book, Lermontov does warn against simplemindedness when considering his book with a swipe at Russian readers: "Our audience is still so young and simple-hearted, it wouldn't recognize a fable if there weren't a moral at the end of the story. It doesn't anticipate jokes, it doesn't have a feel for irony; it is simply badly educated. It doesn't yet know that overt abuse has neither a place in proper society, nor in a proper book; that the contemporary intellect has devised sharper weapons, almost invisible, but nonetheless deathly, which, under the clothing of flattery, deliver an irresistible and decisive blow."

What is abundantly clear is that, irony or no irony, the tsar wasn't pleased with either the hero or the "hero." When *A Hero of Our Time* was published, the tsar famously disparaged the work in a letter to his wife, dated June 1840:

I have now read and finished the "Hero." I find the second volume odious and quite worthy to be fashionable [à la mode] as it is the same gallery of despicable, exaggerated characters that one finds in fashionable foreign novels. It is such novels that debauch morals and distort characters, and whilst one hears such caterwauling with disgust, it always leaves one painfully half-convinced that the world is only composed of such people whose best actions apparently are inspired only by abominable or impure motives. What then is the result? Contempt or hatred of humanity. Is that the aim of our life on earth? One is only too disposed to be hypochondriac or misanthropic. So what is the use, by painting such portraits, of encouraging these tendencies? I therefore repeat my view that the author suffers from a most depraved spirit, and his talents are pathetic. The Captain's character is nicely sketched. In the beginning to read the story I had hoped, and was rejoicing, that he was the Hero of our Times. In his class there are indeed many more truly worthy of this title than those too commonly dignified with it. The (Independent) Caucasian Corps must surely number many of them, whom one gets to know only too rarely, but such a hope is not to be fulfilled in this book, and M. Lermontov was unable to develop the noble and simple character (of the Captain). He is replaced by wretched and uninteresting people, who—proving to be tiresome—would have been far better ignored and thus not provoke one's disgust.[6]

In addition to the tsar's disdain, Lermontov's hero—given a character of such terrific vices and virtues—received a mixed but vigorous reception by reading audiences when it emerged in 1840. And Pechorin's personage is so clearly wrought that, it seems, the public and various critics jumped to the conclusion that the book was largely autobiographical. Indeed, Lermontov had also spent time in the military in the Caucasus, and, given his poems, was also subject to the cynical inclinations of his generation. In his poem "Meditation" of 1838, he writes, "I look upon our generation with sorrow! Its future is either empty or dark . . . And life already tires us, like flat path that leads nowhere ..." Lermontov was not so terribly different from his hero in life experience and outlook, but he was resistant to such a facile reading of the book and writes in his preface, "Not long ago, several readers, and some journals even, succumbed to the misfortune of believing in the literal meanings of the words in this book. Some were awfully offended, in all seriousness, at the fact that they were presented with such an unprincipled person as the 'hero of our time'; indeed, others very shrewdly observed that the author had painted his own portrait and the portraits of his acquaintances ... That sorry, old ruse!"

Such defenses on the part of Lermontov need not concern us too much nearly two hundred years later. Indeed, that they both served in the Caucasus, and that they both fought in duels gives them much in common. For Pechorin, duels and Russian roulette bring about questions that are central to the book, and indeed central to life: "Is there such thing as predestination? ... And if there is definitely such thing as predestination—why were we given free will, and reason? Why should we atone for our actions?" In this book, and in real life, the duel is a manifestation of such questions. And of course, duels were meant to be the stuff of honor and heroics, and yet so many duels in Russia at the time were fought over petty disagreements—if not out of sheer boredom. More heroes doing unheroic things in an age of cynicism. Smaller ironies among one great big one: we lead our lives as though we have choice in our actions and responsibility for these actions, but is "the fate of a man written in the sky" (as Pechorin and his friends discuss in "The Fatalist")?

What is eerie is that not only did Pechorin and Lermontov share experiences and a troubled sense of purpose, but there is a duel scene in *A Hero of Our Time* that almost perfectly describes Lermontov's own death a year or so after the novel emerged. Prince Alexander Vasilchikov, eyewitness to this fateful duel on July 15, 1841, between Lermontov and his opponent Martynov, whom Lermontov had apparently insulted, described the scene of the poet's death thus:

At that moment, and for the last time, I glanced at him and I will never forget the calm, almost gay, expression which played upon the poet's face in front of the barrel of the pistol already directed at him. Martynov approached the barrier with rapid steps and fired. Lermontov fell as if he had been cut down on the spot, without making a movement either forward or backward, without even succeeding in putting his hand to where he had been hurt, as those who have been wounded or grazed usually do. We rushed up. There was a smoking wound in his right side and in his left side he was bleeding: the bullet had gone through his heart and lungs . . . As if it were today, I recall a strange episode of that fateful evening; our wait in the field beside the corpse of Lermontov continued a very long time, because drivers, on the example of the doctor's courage, refused one by one to come out to carry the body of the slain man. Night came on and the downpour was unceasing . . . Suddenly we heard the distant sound of horses' hooves along the path where the body was lying and, in order to drag it out of the way, we tried lifting it; from this movement, as usually happens, air was expelled from the lungs, but with such a sound that it seemed to us that it was a living cry of pain and for a short while we were certain that Lermontov was still alive.[7]

This gives new meaning to composer Balakirev's suggestion that Russians travel to the Caucasus to "breathe in Lermontov."

Lermontov's life was short but reads like Romantic literature. He was unlucky in life and in love. He was born in Moscow in 1814 and grew up in the province of Penza with his grandmother. His mother had died three years after his birth and his grandmother, by all accounts, was overprotective and possessive of him. He was a shy and idealistic youth and when he was sickly as a child, his grandmother took him to the Caucasus to improve his health. This would be Lermontov's first exposure to the land he so admired.

At fourteen years of age he moved with his grandmother to Moscow and attended Moscow University Pension for the

Nobility and went on to study for a few more years at the university. Afterward he entered the St. Petersburg's Guards' School and graduated in 1834. Meanwhile, Lermontov suffered many disappointments, including the death of his father, from whom he had become estranged thanks to his grandmother. His poem "The Terrible Fate of Father and Son" describes the poet's feelings about this event. The young Lermontov's love affairs were also plagued by disappointments. The central object of his affections was named Varavara Lopukhina, who is said to have been "pleasant, clever, bright as the day and ravishing." Lermontov wrote poems to her and made drawings of her but she would marry someone else. Writer and literary historian Janko Lavrin describes Lermontov in particularly vivid tones: "His need of love, 'romantic' and otherwise, was unusually intense. But so were his disappointments . . . Lermontov swallowed his hurt pride; and touchy as he was he never forgave nor forgot . . . Lermontov was thus compelled to develop at an early age a cold and flippantly ironical attitude toward women simply as a safeguard . . ."

But to dismiss Lermontov as a romantic poseur in melodramatic episodes is unfair, and his biographer Laurence Kelly writes that the young writer "[I]n heart-searching letters . . . confessed to a melancholy that was more than a fashionably romantic pose. Behind the masque of social gaiety there was a young man still in his teens, perplexed and unsure, 'unfit for society,' 'seeking impressions, any impressions,' tortured by the secret consciousness that 'I shall end life as a contemptible person . . .' "[8]

Until the mid-1830s, Lermontov's poetry addresses his personal concerns—loneliness, love, the loss of his parents—but he would soon turn to larger themes, both social and political. After leaving cadet school, he lived in St. Petersburg for a few years, and in 1837 he wrote the poem "Death of a Poet," which charged the imperial court with mistreating Pushkin and causing his death. It was then that he was arrested, demoted, and sent to the Caucasus to serve with Russian forces in their struggles against the mountain tribes.

"Death of a Poet" marks the start of a most productive period in Lermontov's career as a writer. Between 1837 and 1840, while Lermontov alternated between stints in St. Petersburg and the Caucasus mountains, he wrote *The Demon, The Novice,* and *A Hero of Our Time,* as well as many poems. After his second Caucasian posting, he returned and asked for permission to leave the army to devote himself to his writing. He was denied. In 1841, he was sent again to the Caucasus, where he died in the duel with Martynov. Upon Lermontov's death, Tsar Nicholas the First is purported to have reacted by saying: "a dog's death for a dog." Such were the times for this literary hero.

Translating Lermontov requires a linguistic zoom lens—while working closely one must regularly pull back to see a larger picture of words. The beauty of his work lies at the level of the sentence and the paragraph. Lermontov is not a writer whose words are so carefully chosen that the translator must agonize to get each syllable pitch-perfect. But faced with the task of translating *A Hero of Our Time,* I did so anyway, out of a sense of fidelity. I followed his every clause carefully, keen to avoid assumptions that can be so easily made in working with writing of a Romantic bent. But most of all, this close reading makes for magic in a translation—in focusing on the building blocks of a text, piling words on top of each other just so, something emerges, an essence that the translator hasn't forced. As Maurice Baring wrote in 1914: "[W]hen you read Pushkin, you think: 'How perfectly and how simply that is said! How in the world did he do it?' You admire the 'magic hand of chance.' In reading Lermontov at his simplest and best, you do not think about the style at all, you simply respond to what is said, and the style escapes notice in its absolute appropriateness."

Lermontov wasn't a master stylist, he was a master storyteller. That's not to say that the quality of the prose is lacking but that his writing is very fluent—not meant to be paused over for any great length of time. A reader needn't look for surprising combinations of words. Lermontov's language is constantly moving—a motion that becomes clear to a translator only upon achieving enough pace to feel the momentum of his writing. As Eikhenbaum wrote: "*A Hero of Our Time* looks like the first 'light' book; a book in which formal problems are concealed beneath careful motivation and which, therefore, was able to create the illusion of 'naturalness' and to arouse an interest in pure reading."[9] The naturalness to which he refers is a very true characterization of Lermontov's writing—the author strived to avoid archaic turns of phrase, and easily captures the voices of the various personages. This is the translator's challenge here: to preserve his nineteenth-century idiom but to avoid anything that seems obsolete to a contemporary reader; to capture the various voices in the novel without too many cultural contortions; to match his rhythms, from paragraph to paragraph; and, above all, to disappear so that the reader may swiftly move through the book and its mountain story. Yes, he tends to repeat words and phrases in this book, and yes, he seems to have a very simplistic palette when it comes to describing colors, and yes, the sun appears from behind cold, snowy, or dark-blue peaks many times over the course of the novel. But his is a feat of narrative, a romping story about a dislikable man who captures your whole attention with his manifold contradictions.

NATASHA RANDALL

NOTES

1. Belinsky, V. G. *Notes of the Fatherland* (St. Peterburg: 1841), vol. XIV, pp. 45–46.
2. Eikhenbaum, B. M. *Lermontov: A Study in Literary-Historical Evaluation* (Ann Arbor: Ardis, 1981), p. 171.
3. Garrard, John. "Old Wine in New Bottles: The Legacy of Lermontov" in *Poetica Slavica: Studies in Honour of Zbigniew Folejewski,* edited by J. Douglas Clayton and Gunter

Acknowledgments

I am particularly grateful to the following people and institutions for their invaluable support of this translation: Nikoloz Japaridze, Eugene Ostashevsky, Adrian Pascu-Tulbure, James Potts, Jane Tozer, and Donald Rayfield, with particular thanks to Katie Kotting, Gordon Wallace, and the Hawthornden Writer's Retreat.

Suggestions for Further Reading

Barratt, Andrew, and A. D. P. Briggs. *A Wicked Irony: The Rhetoric of Lermontov's* A Hero of Our Time (Bristol Classics Press, Bristol, 1989).

Eikhenbaum, Boris. *Lermontov: A Study in Literary-Historical Evaluation* (trans. Ray Parrott and Harry Weber, Ardis, Ann Arbor, 1981).

Freeborn, Richard. *"A Hero of Our Time"* in *The Rise of the Russian Novel* (Cambridge University Press, Cambridge, 1973).

Garrard, John G. *Mikhail Lermontov* (Twayne Publishers, Boston, 1982).

Gifford, Henry. *The Hero of His Time; A Theme in Russian Literature* (Edward Arnold and Co., London, 1950).

Gilroy, Marie. *Lermontov's Ironic Vision* (Birmingham Slavonic Monographs No. 19, published by the Department of Russian Language and Literature, University of Birmingham, 1989).

Kelly, Laurence. *Lermontov: Tragedy in the Caucasus* (Constable and Company, London, 1977).

Lavrin, Janko. *Lermontov* (Bowes and Bowes, London, 1959).

Lermontov, Mikhail Yurievich. "The Demon" in *Narrative Poems by Alexander Pushkin and by Mikhail Lermontov* (trans. Charles Johnston, Random House, New York, 1983).

Lermontov, Mikhail Yurievich. "The Novice" in *Narrative Poems by Alexander Pushkin and by Mikhail Lermontov* (trans. Charles Johnston, Random House, New York, 1983).

Mersereau, John. *Mikhail Lermontov* (Southern Illinois University Press, Carbondale, 1962).

Reid, Robert. *Lermontov's* A Hero of Our Time (Bristol Classical Press, Bristol, 1997).

SEA OF
AZOV

Kerch
Taman
R. Kuban
KUBAN
R. Laba
Stavropol

Gelendzhik

CAUCASUS MOUNTAINS

BLACK SEA

- - - - The Line
—·—· Georgian Military Highway

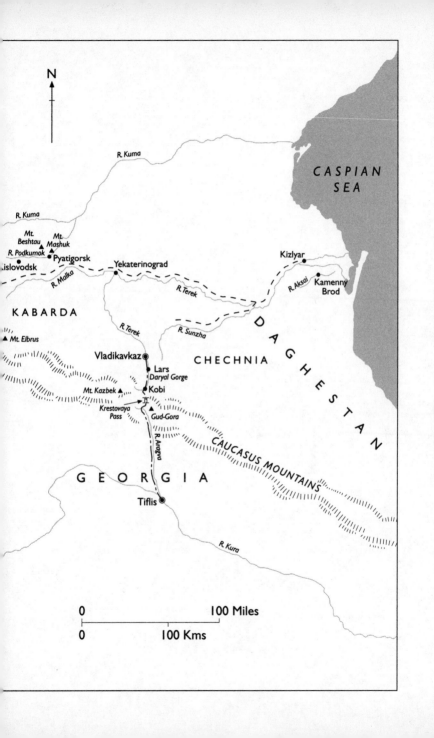

A Hero of Our Time

Foreword

A foreword is both the first and the last thing to a book: it serves either to explain the aims of the work, or to justify it and respond to its critics. But usually, the reader is not involved in moral purpose or journalistic offensives, and hence they don't read forewords. This is a shame, especially for our country. Our audience is still so young and simple-hearted, it wouldn't recognize a fable if there weren't a moral at the end of the story. It doesn't anticipate jokes, it doesn't have a feel for irony; it is simply badly educated. It doesn't yet know that overt abuse has neither a place in proper society, nor in a proper book; that the contemporary intellect has devised sharper weapons, almost invisible, but nonetheless deathly, which, under the clothing of flattery, deliver an irresistible and decisive blow. Our audience is like a provincial person, who overhears a conversation between two diplomats belonging to enemy sovereignties, and is left convinced that they are both betraying their governments for the sake of mutual, affectionate friendship.

Not long ago, several readers, and some journals even, succumbed to the misfortune of believing in the literal meanings of the words in this book. Some were awfully offended, in all seriousness, at the fact that they were presented with such an unprincipled person as the "hero of our time"; indeed, others very shrewdly observed that the author had painted his own portrait and the portraits of his acquaintances . . . That sorry, old ruse! But, apparently, Rus'[1] is a creature in whom everything is constantly being renewed except nonsense such as this. The most magical of our magical fairy tales can barely escape the reproach that it is an attempt at insulting certain people!

A Hero of Our Time, my gracious sirs, is indeed a portrait, but not of one person: it is a portrait composed of the flaws of our whole generation in their fullest development. You will tell me that a person cannot be as nasty as this, but I'll say to you that you have believed in the possible existences of every other tragic and romantic scoundrel, so why won't you believe in the actuality of Pechorin? Since you have admired much more terrible and monstrous figments of imagination, why can't you find mercy in yourselves for this character, just as a figment of imagination? Could it be that there is more truth to him, than you might like . . . ?

Will you say that morality gains nothing from all of this? Forgive me. Enough people have been fed on sweets: their guts have rotted from them. What is needed is a bitter medicine, the pungent truth. But do not think now that the author of this book has had the proud impulse to remedy human flaws. God cure him of such audacity! It simply amused him to paint the contemporary person, one that he understands, and to his misfortune has come across too often.

PART ONE

I

BELA

I was traveling post from Tiflis. The entire load of my cart consisted of one valise of average size, half-filled with my travel notes about Georgia. The majority of these, luckily for you, were lost; but the valise with the rest of my things, luckily for me, remained intact.

The sun was just beginning to hide behind snowy peaks when I entered the Koyshaursky Valley. The Ossetian cart driver sang songs at full voice as he tirelessly urged the horses onward, so that we might succeed in climbing Koyshaursky Mountain before nightfall. What a glorious place, this valley! On every side there are unassailable mountains and reddish promontories, hung with green ivy and crowned with clumps of plane trees; there are yellow precipices, covered with the lines of gullies; and right up high: a gold fringe of snow. Below, the Aragva River, having gathered another nameless rivulet which noisily unearthed itself from a black and gloomy chasm, extends like a silver thread, glittering like a scaly snake.

We arrived at the foot of the Koyshaursky Mountain and stopped at a *dukhan*.[1] Two dozen or so Georgians and other mountain dwellers were crowded noisily there. Nearby, a caravan of camels had stopped for a night's shelter. I was supposed to hire some bullocks to drag my cart up this forsaken mountain, because it was autumn already, there was black ice, and this slope was about two *versts*[2] in length.

There was nothing else to be done so I hired the six bullocks and a few Ossetians. One of them hoisted my valise onto his shoulders; the others started to prod the bullocks using their voices alone.

Behind my cart, another was being pulled by a foursome of bullocks as though it took no effort, even though it was full to the brim. This disparity surprised me. The owner walked behind his cart, smoking a little Kabardian pipe plated in silver. He wore an officer's frock coat without epaulets and a shaggy Circassian hat. He seemed about fifty years old; the dark complexion of his face showed that it was long acquainted with the Transcaucasian sun, but the premature graying of his mustache didn't correspond with his solid gait and bright appearance. I walked up to him and bowed; he silently returned the bow and pushed out an enormous cloud of smoke.

"It seems you and I will be traveling companions?"

He bowed again silently.

"Might you be going to Stavropol?"

"Yes, indeed . . . on official business."

"Tell me, if you would, why is your heavy cart being pulled easily by four bullocks, when mine, which is empty, can barely be moved by six beasts with the help of these Ossetians?"

He smiled slyly and looked at me with emphasis.

"You have only recently arrived in the Caucasus, perhaps?"

"About a year ago," I replied.

He smiled a second time.

"Well . . . what?"

"Yes! What awful rogues, these Asiatics! You think they're urging those bullocks with what they're saying? Devil knows what they're crying out. The bulls, though, they understand them. You could yoke twenty to your cart even, and the bullocks still wouldn't move as long as they cry out like that . . . Awful cheats! But what do you expect of them? . . . They love to make off with the money of passersby . . . the spoiled little swindlers! You'll see, they have yet to ask you for vodka money. I know them, you see, and won't have them lead me along!"

"And have you served here long?"

"I served here before under Alexei Petrovich," he replied, assuming a dignified air. "When he arrived at the front I was a second lieutenant," he added, "and under him I received two promotions for action against the mountain-dwellers."

"And now, you are . . . ?"

"Now I consider myself to be in the battalion of the third line. And you, might I be so bold as to ask . . . ?"

I told him.

My conversation with the man ended, and we continued in silence one after the other. We found snow at the summit of the mountain. The sun set, and night followed day without interval, as is often the way in the south; but thanks to the tint of the snows we were easily able to make out the road, which continued up the mountain, though not as steeply as before. I gave orders to deposit my valise on the cart, exchange the bullocks for horses, and for the last time, I looked back down to see the valley. But a thick fog had covered it completely, having surged in waves up from the gorge, and not one sound from below could now fly up and reach our hearing. The Ossetians noisily clustered around me and requested something for vodka, but the staff captain shouted at them so menacingly that they ran off instantly.

"What a people!" he said. "They can't even name the word for bread in Russian, but they've learned to say 'Officer, give us something for our vodka!' I think even the Tatars are a better sort—at least they don't drink . . ."

One *verst* remained to the station. It was quiet all around us, so quiet that you could follow the flight of a mosquito by its buzzing. The deep gorge to our left was growing black; beyond it, the dark-blue summit of the mountain faced us, pitted with creases, covered in layers of snow, and silhouetted against a pale band of sky above the horizon, which was conserving the last reflection of the sunset. Stars began to sparkle in the dark sky, and strangely it seemed to me that they were a great deal higher than they are in the north. Bare, black rocks stuck out on both sides of the road; in some places shrubs peeped out from under the snow, but not one dry leaf stirred. It was cheering to hear the snorting of a tired *troika*[3] and the uneven rattling of a small Russian bell in the midst of this dead dream of nature.

"Tomorrow will be glorious weather!" I said. The staff captain didn't say a word and pointed his finger at the high mountain that was rising in front of us.

"What is it?"

"Gud Mountain."

"And what is that?"

"See how it's smoking."

And it was true, Gud Mountain was smoking. Light little currents of cloud were creeping down its slopes, and a black storm cloud sat at its summit, so black that it looked like a blot on the dark sky.

We could just make out the posting house, the roofs of its surrounding *saklyas,*[4] and their welcoming little fires twinkling at us, when suddenly a damp, cold wind blew in, a droning sound started in the gorge, and a drizzle began. I barely managed to throw on my felt cloak[5] as snow began to pour down. I looked over at the staff captain in deference . . .

"We'll have to spend the night here," he said with vexation. "You'll never get across the mountain in this sort of snowstorm. Well? Have there been any avalanches on the Krestovaya?" he asked the cart driver.

"No, there haven't," replied the cart driver. "But there's a lot hanging up there—a lot."

We were led off to spend the night in a smoky *saklya* since there was no bedchamber for travelers stopping at the station. I invited my fellow traveler to drink a glass of tea with me, for I had with me a cast-iron tea-kettle—the one and only comfort on my travels in the Caucasus.

The *saklya* was pinned to the rock-face on one side. Three slippery, wet steps led to its door. I felt my way through the entrance, and stumbled upon a cow (to these people, a cowshed is easily substituted for servants' quarters). I didn't know where to put myself: there were sheep bleating in one corner, a dog was growling in the other. Fortunately, a dim light shone from the side and helped me to find another opening, which resembled a door. It gave onto a rather entertaining scene: a wide *saklya,* the roof of which was propped up on two soot-covered posts and filled with people. A little fire chattered, which had been laid on the bare earth in the center of the room; smoke was being forced back through an opening in the roof by the wind, and it unfurled throughout the room in such a dense shroud that I couldn't make out my surroundings for a long time. Two old women, a multitude of children, and a lean Georgian sat by the fire, all of them in rags. There was nothing to do but take shelter by the fire and begin to smoke our pipes. Soon the tea-kettle started to fizz with friendliness.

"A wretched people!" I said to the staff captain, pointing to our dirty hosts, who were looking at us silently, sort of dumbfounded.

"Such dim-witted folk!" he replied. "Can you believe it? They can't do anything, aren't capable of any kind of learning! At least our Kabardin or Chechens, though they are robbers, and paupers too, they make up for it by being daredevils. But these ones have no affinity for weapons: you won't find a decent dagger on any of them. Genuine Ossetians!"

"Were you in Chechnya for a long time?"

"Yes, I was posted there for about ten years with my company in the fortress at Kamenny Brod—do you know it?"

"Heard of it."

"Well, old fellow, let me tell you, we were fed up with those bandits! Now, thank God, it's quieter. But there was a time when if you took a hundred steps beyond the ramparts, there was a shaggy devil lying in wait. If you even stopped to gape, you'd have a lasso around your neck or a bullet in the back of your head. Oh, they're clever ones . . . !"

"So, you've had many adventures I would think?" I said, my curiosity excited.

"How could I not?! Indeed I have . . ."

Here he started to pluck at the left side of his mustache, hung his head, and became pensive. I wanted terribly to extract some little story from him—a desire characteristic of all those who travel and write. Meanwhile, the tea was brewed;

I took two little traveling glasses from my valise, filled them and set one of them in front of him. He took a sip and said, as if to himself: "Yes, I have!" This exclamation gave me more hope. I know that old soldiers of the Caucasus love to talk, to tell tales; and they rarely get the chance to do so. This one had been in post for five-odd years somewhere in the sticks with his military company, and not once in those five years did anyone say "good day" to him (because a sergeant-major always says "Preserve your health"). And there was plenty to chat about: the local peoples were savage, a curious people; there was danger present every day; miraculous events occurred; and you couldn't help but regret that so little of this gets recorded.

"You wouldn't like to add some rum?" I said to my interlocutor. "I have white rum from Tiflis. It's cold outside now."

"No, thank you sir, I don't drink."

"Is that so?"

"Yes, that's right. I've taken an oath. You see, once when I was still a second lieutenant, we had a little too much to drink between us, and at night the alarm sounded. So we merrily turned out in front of the soldiers in our merry state, and we got it in the neck when Alexei Petrovich found out. Good God how furious he was! He nearly had us court-martialed. There's no doubt that if you spend a whole year without seeing a soul, and you add vodka to that, you'll be a missing person!"

Hearing this, I almost lost hope.

"Yes, and there's the Circassians," he continued. "As soon as they drink up the *bouza*[6] at a wedding or funeral, the knives come out. Once I barely managed to walk away intact, even though I was the guest of a peaceable prince."[7]

"How did that happen?"

"Well," he packed his pipe, drew on it, and began his account, "allow me to explain. I was posted at the fortress near the Terek River with my company—almost five years ago. Once, in the autumn, a transport arrived with provisions. And in that transport was an officer—a young man, of about twenty-five years. He presents himself to me in full uniform and announces that he has orders to remain with me at the fortress. He was such a thin and fair thing, the full-dress uniform he wore was so new, that I guessed then and there that he hadn't been long in the Caucasus.

" 'Would I be right in saying,' I asked him, 'that you have been transferred here from Russia?'

" 'Indeed, Mr. Staff Captain,' he replied.

"I took him by the hand and said: 'Very pleased, very pleased to meet you. You will find it somewhat tedious . . . but you and I will live together at ease. Yes, please, call me simply Maxim Maximych, and please—why this full uniform? Present yourself to me in your military cap.'

"They took him to his quarters and he settled at the fortress."

"And what was his name?" I asked Maxim Maximych.

"His name was . . . Grigory Alexandrovich Pechorin. A wonderful fellow, I dare say. Only a little strange too. For example, he would spend the whole day hunting in a drizzling cold that would freeze and exhaust most others to the bone—but to him it was nothing. And then, at other times, he would be sitting in his room, and the wind would blow, and he'd swear to you that he was catching cold. A shutter would bang and he'd shiver and go pale. But I can attest that he would go out after wild boar, one on one. Sometimes whole hours would go by without a word from him, and then other times, he'd start telling a story, and immediately your belly would ache from laughing . . . Yes, he had a good deal of great oddities, and he must have been a rich man—he had so many expensive things!"

"Did he stay with you long?" I asked again.

"Almost a year. But that year is certainly memorable for me; he created a lot of trouble for me, but that is not why I mention it. It seems, in fact, that there is a type of person who is destined from birth to be subjected to various unusual things!"

"Unusual?" I exclaimed with a look of curiosity, helping him to more tea.

"Well, I'll explain. About six *verst*s from the fortress lived a peaceable prince.[8] His young son, a boy of about fifteen, took to visiting us every day for one reason or another. Grigory Alexandrovich and I spoiled him, we did. And he was such a rascal, and nimble at whatever he did—whether he was picking up a hat at full gallop or firing a rifle. There was just one thing about him that was no good: he had a terrible weakness for money. Once, for a laugh, Grigory Alexandrovich promised him a gold piece if he would steal the best goat in his father's herd. And what do you think? The very next night he dragged it in by its horns. But if we ever thought to tease him, his eyes would fill with blood, and he'd be at the ready with his dagger.

"'Eh, Azamat, don't lose your head now,' I told him, 'you'll get it cut off!'

"Once the old prince himself came and invited us to a wedding. He was giving away his eldest daughter's hand in marriage. Given I was his *kunak*,[9] I couldn't, you know, decline—he is a Tatar after all. So we went. We were met at the *aul*[10] by a lot of dogs barking loudly. The women, having seen us, hid themselves. Those whose faces we could see were far from beautiful.

"'I had a much higher opinion of Circassian women,' said Grigory Alexandrovich.

"'Wait a moment!' I replied, laughing. I had something in mind.

"A crowd of people had gathered in the prince's *saklya*. The Asiatics, you know, have a custom of inviting everyone and anyone to their weddings. They received us with every honor, and led us to their special rooms. I, however, did not forget to note where they put our horses—you know, in the event of unforeseen circumstances."

"How do they celebrate weddings?" I asked the staff captain.

"Oh, in the usual way. At the beginning the *Mullah* reads them something from the Koran. Then he gives presents to the young couple and all their relatives. They eat, drink *bouza* and then they begin trick riding—and there's always one, some dirty ragamuffin on a lousy and lame nag, who poses, plays the clown, and makes the good company laugh. Then, when it gets dark, in the special rooms, what we would call a 'ball' starts up. A poor little old man strums away on a . . . I forget what it is in their language . . . well, yes, it's something like our *balalaika*.[11] The girls and the young men stand in two rows, facing each other, and they clap their palms together and sing. And then one of the girls and one of the men come forward into the middle and start to address each other in sung verse with whatever comes to them (any old thing), and the others join in with the chorus. Pechorin and I sat in the honored seats, and then our host's youngest daughter, a girl of sixteen, approached him, and sang him a . . . how can I put it? A sort of compliment."

"And what did she sing—do you remember?"

"Yes, it seems it was something like, 'Our young *dzhigits*[12] are strapping, and their caftans are covered in silver, but the young Russian officer is more strapping than they, and the galloon[13] he wears is in gold. He is like a poplar among them— only he won't grow; he doesn't bloom in our garden.'

"Pechorin stood up, bowed to her, put his hand to his head and to his heart, and asked me to reply to her; I know how to speak like them and translated his answer.

"When she walked away from us, I whispered to Grigory Alexandrovich:

"'Well, what do you think of her?'

"'Enchanting!' he replied. 'What is her name?'

"'Her name is Bela,' I replied.

"And indeed, she was fine: tall, slim, with black eyes like a hill chamois[14] that cast a look straight into your soul. Pechorin, in his reverie, didn't take his eyes off her, and she looked over at him from under her brow fairly often too. But it wasn't only Pechorin who admired the winning princess: from the corner of the room two other eyes were looking at her, fixed and fiery. I looked over and recognized my old acquaintance Kazbich. He was, you understand, neither peaceable nor unpeaceable as it were. There were lots of suspicions about him, even though he wasn't ever discovered making even one bit of mischief. Sometimes, he would bring sheep to us at the fortress, and he sold them cheaply—he never haggled. You would give what he asked—come what may, he wouldn't bend. They say that he loves to roam along the Kuban River with the *abreks,*[15] and to tell the truth, he had a thievish snout on him. He was small, spindly, wide-shouldered . . . And then his cunning—he was as cunning as a demon! His *beshmet*[16] was always in tatters and patches, but his weapon was in silver. And his horse was famous in the whole Kabarde—you couldn't even dream of a better horse. Not for nothing that all the horsemen envied him—and they tried to steal him more than once but never managed it. I can see that horse even now: black as jet, legs like bow-strings, and eyes no worse than Bela's—and what strength! He'll gallop at least 50 *verst*s—and he's well-trained too—runs like a dog after his master, and knows the man's voice even! They say that Kazbich never ties him up. What a perfect horse for a thief!

"That evening, Kazbich was as sullen as ever, and I noticed that he had a chain mail shirt under his *beshmet.* 'He's wearing this chain mail shirt for a reason,' I thought. 'He has probably laid a plan.'

"It became stuffy in the *saklya,* and I went out into the fresh air to revive myself. Night had already fallen on the mountains, and a thundercloud began to wander along the ravines.

"It occurred to me to look in on our horses in the shelter, to see if they had feed, and besides, caution is never a hindrance—after all, I had a splendid horse. The Kabardin have, more than once, looked at it and repeated ingratiatingly, 'Yakshi tkhe, chek yakshi!'[17]

"I steal along the fence and suddenly I hear voices; I immediately recognized one voice: it was the rake Azamat, the son of our host. The other spoke more thinly and more quietly. 'What are they talking about?' I thought. 'Not about my horse surely . . .' So, I sat down by the fence and began listening, trying not to miss a word. Occasionally, the noise of singing and the sound of talking would fly over from the *saklya,* deafening this conversation that was so interesting to me.

" 'Splendid horse you have!' said Azamat. 'If I was master

of the house and owned a herd of three hundred mares, then I would give you half of them for your steed, Kazbich!'

"'Ah! Kazbich!' I thought and remembered the chain mail shirt.

"'Yes,' replied Kazbich, after a certain silence, 'you won't find one like it in the whole of the Kabarde. Once—this was beyond the Terek River—I was riding with the *abreks* to re-capture herds from the Russians. We'd had no luck and scat-tered, each in his own direction. Four Cossacks rushed up behind me; I heard the yells of the *gyaurs*[18] behind me and I saw a thick wood in front of me. I sat low to the saddle, entrusted myself to Allah, and for the first time in my life I insulted my horse with lashings of my whip. Like a bird he dived between branches; sharp thorns tore my clothes, dry elm branches beat me across the face. My horse leapt over tree stumps, ripped shrubs apart with his breast. Perhaps I should have abandoned him at the forest's edge, and hidden myself on foot in the woods, but I was sorry to part with him—and the prophet rewarded me. Several bullets squealed over my head; I could hear the Cossacks in hot pursuit . . . Suddenly, before me there was a gully; my steed paused for thought—and jumped. His hind hooves had come away from the opposite bank, and he hung there from his front legs. I cast away the reins and threw myself into the gully; this saved my horse: he sprang out. The Cossacks saw all this, only not one of them came down to look for me. They prob-ably thought that I had killed myself, and I heard them give up trying to catch my horse. My heart was bleeding. I crawled through thick grasses along the length of the gully—and then I see: the forest had ended, several Cossacks are riding into a clearing and then, running right up to them is Karagyoz.[19] They all threw themselves at him with a cry; they chased him for a long, long time, and twice one of them almost managed to throw a lasso around his neck. I started to tremble, cast my eyes down, and began praying. After a few moments I lift my eyes and see: my Karagyoz is flying, his tail fluttering as free as the wind, and the *gyaurs* are far behind, one after the other moving along the steppe on worn-out horses. By Allah, it's the truth, the real truth! I sat in my gully until late into the night. Suddenly, what do you think happens, Azamat? In the darkness I hear a horse running along the gully's edge, snorting, neighing, and beating his hooves on the ground. I recognized the voice of my Karagyoz: it was him—my lifelong friend! . . . Since then, we have never separated.'

"And I could hear how he patted the smooth neck of his steed with his hand, giving him various affectionate names.

"'If I had a herd of a thousand mares,' said Azamat, 'then I'd give them all to you for your Karagyoz.'

"'*Yok*,[20] not interested,' replied Kazbich indifferently.

"'Listen, Kazbich,' Azamat said, fawning at him, 'you're a kind person, you're a brave *dzhigit,* but my father is afraid of the Russians and won't let me into the mountains. Give me your horse, and I will do anything you want. I will steal my father's best rifle or saber for you, whatever you desire— and his saber is real *gurda.*[21] Hold the blade in your hand, and it will stick itself into a body—a chain mail shirt like yours wouldn't stand a chance.'

"Kazbich said nothing.

"'The first time I saw your horse,' continued Azamat, 'he was turning circles and jumping underneath you, flaring his nostrils, with splinters of flint flying from his hooves, and something I can't explain happened in my soul—it has made me weary ever since. I look at my father's best steeds with scorn, I am ashamed to be seen on them, and a longing has seized me, and I have sat for whole days on the cliff edge in anguish, while thoughts come to me every minute of your jet-black horse with his elegant gait, with his smooth, arrow-straight spine. He once looked me in the eye with his bold eyes, as though he wanted to utter a word. I will die, Kazbich, if you don't sell him to me!' said Azamat, with a trembling voice.

"I could hear that he had started to weep—but I must tell you that Azamat was a very persistent little boy, and some- times, nothing would drive away his tears, even when he was younger.

"The reaction to his tears sounded a bit like laughter.

"'Listen!' said Azamat with a firm voice. 'You'll see, I'll resolve everything. If you want I'll steal my sister for you. How she dances! How she sings! And she embroiders with gold—it's a marvel! No one has ever had such a wife—even the Turkish *Padishah*[22] . . . Do you want me to get her? Wait for me tomorrow night over there, in the ravine, by the stream. I'll go past with her on our way to the next *aul*—and she is yours. Isn't Bela at least worth your steed? Don't tell me Bela isn't worth your steed?'

"Kazbich said nothing for a long, long time; finally, instead of an answer, he struck up an ancient song in a low voice:

> The many lovely girls of our land,
> their dark eyes sparkle with stars and,
> Love them: a sweet and enviable destiny,
> Better though is courage and liberty.
> Gold will buy you four wives yes,
> But a spirited horse has no price,
> In a wind-storm on the Steppe he'll abide,
> He won't betray you, he won't lie.*[23]

"In vain, Azamat begged him to agree, he wept and flattered him, and swore oaths. In the end, Kazbich impatiently cut him short:

"'Away with you, you silly little boy! Where would you be going on my horse? He'd throw you off within the first three paces, and you'd break your head on a rock.'

"'Me!?' cried Azamat in a fury, and the iron of the child's dagger began to ring against the chain mail shirt. A strong hand pushed him swiftly off, and the boy struck so hard against the wattle fencing that it started to sway.

"'Let the games begin!' I thought, and rushed into the stable, bridled our horses, and led them out into the back courtyard. After just two minutes, there was a terrible commotion

---

* I beg the reader's pardon for putting Kazbich's song into verse, when it had been relayed to me in prose—but such a habit is second nature to me.

in the *saklya*. This is what had happened: Azamat had run inside with a torn *beshmet,* saying that Kazbich had tried to knife him. Everyone grabbed up their weapons and leapt out—and the fun began! A cry, a noise, shots; but Kazbich was already mounted, and twirled down the street among the crowd, like a demon, brushing them off with his saber.

" 'Best not to feel the heel of someone else's meal,' I said to Grigory Alexandrovich, catching hold of his arm, 'wouldn't it be better for us to be off now?'

" 'No, wait a moment, let's see how it ends.'

" 'Well, it's likely to end badly. These Asiatics are always like this—they pull out the *bouza,* and the carnage begins!'

"We mounted our horses, and galloped home."

"And what happened to Kazbich?" I asked the staff captain impatiently.

"Well, what do you think happens to his sort?" he replied, drinking the rest of his tea. "He slipped away!"

"Wasn't he wounded?" I asked.

"God only knows! They are hardy, these bandits! I've even seen them in action, and there was one I saw still waving his saber around after he'd been stuck so full of bayonet holes, he was like a sieve."

The staff captain, after a certain silence, stamped his foot on the ground and continued. "I'll never forgive myself for one thing though: the devil possessed me, and when we arrived at the fortress, I recounted everything that I'd heard by the fence to Grigory Alexandrovich. He laughed—so cunning!—and then planned a little something himself."

"What was it? Tell me please."

"Well, there's nothing to be done about it—I've started telling you so I'll have to continue.

"Four days later, Azamat arrives at the fortress. As usual, he called in on Grigory Alexandrovich, who always fed him sweets. I was there. A conversation started up about horses, and Pechorin started to sing the praises of Kazbich's horse: how frisky he was, how beautiful, like a chamois—and well, simply, in his words, there wasn't another like it in the world.

"The little eyes of the Tatar boy started to sparkle, but it was as if Pechorin hadn't noticed. I started to talk about something different, but before you knew it he would deflect the conversation right back to Kazbich's horse. And this story continued itself every time Azamat came to us. Three weeks later, I started to notice that Azamat was turning pale and withering, as happens to characters when love strikes in a novel. How extraordinary!

"And, you see, I only found out about this next bit later: Grigory Alexandrovich had teased him so unmercifully that the boy was almost driven to drown himself. Once he said to him, 'I see, Azamat, that you love this horse to the point of pain—but you're as unlikely to see it as you are the back of your head! Tell me, what would you give to the person who made a present of the horse to you?'

" 'Anything he wanted,' replied Azamat.

" 'In that case, I will get him for you, only on one condition . . . swear you will do what I ask.'

" 'I swear . . . And you swear too!'

" 'Good! I swear you will have the horse. Only in exchange for it, you must give me your sister Bela; Karagyoz will be her bride-money. I hope that this trade will be advantageous to you.'

"Azamat said nothing.

" 'You don't want to? Well, as you like! I thought that you were a man, but you're still a child. It's too soon for you to be riding . . .'

"Azamat blushed.

" 'And what about my father?' he said.

" 'Doesn't he ever go anywhere?'

" 'True . . .'

" 'Are we agreed?'

" 'Agreed,' Azamat whispered, as pale as death. 'But when?'

" 'The next time Kazbich comes here. He has promised to drive a dozen sheep to us. The rest is my business. You'll see, Azamat!'

"So they arranged the matter . . . and truth be told, it was a bad business! Afterward I was saying so to Pechorin and he only replied that a wild Circassian girl should be happy to have as kind a husband as he, because according to their ways, he would be her husband. And that Kazbich is a bandit, who should be punished. You judge for yourself, what could I have said to that? . . . At the time, though, I knew no details of their plot. And then Kazbich arrived one day, asking if we needed any sheep or honey; I ordered him to bring some the next day.

" 'Azamat!' said Grigory Alexandrovich. 'Tomorrow Karagyoz will be in my hands. If Bela isn't here tonight, then you won't set eyes on your horse . . .'

" 'Fine!' said Azamat, and galloped to the *aul*.

"That evening Grigory Alexandrovich armed himself and left the fortress. How they arranged this matter, I don't know— but that night both returned, and the sentry saw a woman across Azamat's saddle, whose hands and feet were bound, and whose head was shrouded in a *yashmak*."[24]

"And the horse?" I asked the staff captain.

"Yes, yes. The day before, Kazbich had arrived early in the morning, having driven a dozen sheep to us for sale. He tied up his horse at the fence and came in to see me. I treated him to tea, because though he was a bandit, he was my *kunak* all the same.

"We started talking about this and that . . . And suddenly I see Kazbich flinch and change countenance. He went to the window: but the window, unfortunately, gave onto the back yard.

" 'What's wrong?' I asked.

" 'My horse! . . . Horse!' he said, trembling all over.

"Indeed, I could clearly hear the trotting of hooves. 'It's true, some Cossack has arrived . . .'

" 'No! *Urus—yaman, yaman!*'[25] he started to bellow and threw himself headlong in their direction, like a wild snow leopard. In two leaps he was already in the courtyard; at the gates of the fortress, the sentry blocked his way with a rifle; he jumped over the rifle and started running down the road . . . Dust spiraled up in the distance—Azamat was galloping off on the spirited Karagyoz. As he ran, Kazbich pulled his rifle out of its case and took a shot. For about a minute he stood there trying to believe his bad luck. After that he began to scream. He struck his rifle against a rock and it broke into fragments, he collapsed onto the ground and began to sob like a child . . . And then, the inhabitants of the fortress gathered around him—but he didn't notice any of them. They stood around, had a chat, and went back. I ordered money to be put down next to him for the sheep—and he didn't touch it, but lay face-down, like a corpse. Can you believe that he lay there like that till late evening and then through the night? . . . It wasn't until the next morning that he came into the fortress and started requesting that the abductor be named. The sentry, who saw Azamat untie the horse and ride off on him, didn't consider it necessary to conceal. At the sound of the name, Kazbich's eyes began to sparkle and he headed for the *aul* of Azamat's father."

"And the father?"

"Yes, well, that's the thing. Kazbich didn't find him—he had gone off somewhere for six days, otherwise how could Azamat have managed to make off with his sister?

"And when the father returned, there was no daughter. And there was no son—the cunning boy, it seems he figured out that he would lose his head if he were caught. So he left: and probably, attached himself to some band of *abreks*. He has laid his head down on the other side of the Terek or the Kuban—and it serves him right!

"I admit that I saw a fair amount of trouble for it too. As soon as I learned that the Circassian girl was with Grigory Alexandrovich, I donned my epaulets and sword, and I went to him.

"He was lying in the front room on a bed, with one arm behind his head, and the other holding an extinguished pipe. The door to the second room was locked, and the key to its lock was missing. I saw all this immediately . . . I started to cough, and to tap my heels at the threshold—but he pretended he hadn't heard.

"'Ensign, sir!' I said as sternly as I could. 'Can you not see that you have a visitor?'

"'Ah, greetings, Maxim Maximych! Would you like a pipe?' he replied, not rising even slightly.

"'Excuse me! I am not Maxim Maximych: I am the staff captain.'

"'All the same. Would you like some tea? If you only knew what worries are troubling me!'

"'I know everything,' I said, having walked up to the bed.

"'All the better: I don't have it in me to recount it.'

"'Ensign, sir, you have committed a misdemeanor, for which I too may have to answer . . .'

"'Come, come! What is the matter? It would seem that we have long split everything in half.'

"'How could you make such jokes? Your sword, if you please!'

"'Mitka, my sword!'

"Mitka brought the sword. Having fulfilled my duty, I sat down on his bed and said: 'Listen Grigory Alexandrovich, admit that it was a bad thing you did.'

"'What was a bad thing?'

"'That you took Bela . . . And as for that rogue Azamat! . . . Come on, admit it,' I said.

"'And what if I like her?'

"Well, what would you have liked me to reply to that? . . . I was at a dead end. However, after a certain length of silence I said to him that if her father started to ask for her, then he'd have to give her back!

"'Totally unnecessary!'

"'And if he finds out she's here?'

"'How will he find out?'

"I was again faced with a dead-end.

"'Listen, Maxim Maximych!' said Pechorin, lifting himself up a little. 'You're a kind fellow, so consider: if we return the savage's daughter to him, he will murder her or sell her. The deed is done, and there's no need to ruin things further—leave her with me, and you can keep my sword . . .'

"'Well, show her to me,' I said.

"'She is behind that door. But just now, I myself tried in vain to see her—she is sitting in the corner, wrapped in a shawl. She isn't talking, isn't looking up—as frightened as a wild chamois. I've engaged our lady-innkeeper; she knows Tatar, she will take care of her and will train her to accept the thought that she is mine, because she isn't going to belong to anyone except me,' he added, banging his fist on the table. And I agreed to that too . . . What else could I do? There are people with whom one must absolutely agree."

"And then?" I asked Maxim Maximych. "Did he really train her to be his or did she wither away in her unwillingness, out of longing for her motherland?"

"For pity's sake, why would she long for her motherland? The same hills are visible from the fortress as from the *aul*—these savages need nothing more than that. And furthermore, every day Grigory Alexandrovich gave her something: for the first few days, she silently and proudly pushed the presents away, which were then passed to the lady-innkeeper, exciting her eloquence. Ah, presents! What a woman will do for some colorful rag! . . . But I digress . . . For a long time Pechorin tussled with her; and in the meantime he learned Tatar, and she started to understand our language. Bit by bit she became accustomed to looking at him, at first furtively, from the side. Still pining, she sang her songs under her breath, so that, sometimes, I also became sad when I listened to her from the adjacent room. I will never forget one scene: I walked past and looked through the window; Bela was sitting on the stove-bench, her head hanging down onto her chest, and Grigory Alexandrovich stood in front of her.

" 'Listen, my *peri*,'[26] he was saying, 'you know that sooner or later you will have to be mine, why do you torture me so? Is it that you love some Chechen? If that is so, then I'll send you home now.' She shuddered just noticeably and shook her head. 'Or,' he continued, 'am I completely hateful to you?' She exhaled. 'Or does your faith prohibit you from loving me?' She paled and said nothing. 'Trust me. Allah is the same for every tribe, and if he allows me to love you, why would he forbid you to requite me with the same?' She looked at him in the face intently, as if she were struck with this new thought; her eyes expressed mistrust and a desire to

be convinced. What eyes! They sparkled as though they were
two pieces of coal. 'Listen, my sweet, good Bela!' continued
Pechorin. 'See how I love you; I am prepared to give anything in order to cheer you up. I want you to be happy. But
if you're going to pine, then I'll die. Tell me, will you be
more cheerful?'

"She became pensive, not lowering her black eyes from
him. And then she smiled affectionately and nodded her
head in a sign of agreement. He took her hand and started to
persuade her to kiss him; she weakly defended herself and
only repeated, 'Pleeze, pleeze, duon't, duon't.' He started to
insist; she trembled, and started to cry.

"'I am your captive,' she was saying, 'your slave. Of course,
you can force me,' and she shed more tears.

"Grigory Alexandrovich struck his fist against his forehead and leapt out into the next room. I went in to see him.
He was pacing sullenly back and forth, with his arms crossed
on his chest.

"'What's the matter, old friend?' I said to him.

"'A devil, not a woman!' he replied. 'Only I'll give you my
honest word, that she will be mine . . .'

"I shook my head.

"'Would you like to bet on it?' he said. 'Give me a week's
time!'

"'Done.'

"We shook on it, and went our separate ways.

"The very next day, he sent a messenger to Kizlyar for
various purchases. There was a multitude of Persian goods
among them, so many that they can't be listed.

"'What do you think, Maxim Maximych,' he said on showing me the gifts, 'will the Asiatic beauty withstand such a
battery?'

"'You don't know Circassian girls,' I replied. 'They are not
at all like Georgian girls, or the Tatar girls from beyond the
Caucasus—not at all. They have their own rules. They are
brought up otherwise.' Grigory Alexandrovich smiled and
started to whistle a marching song.

"Well, it seemed I was right: the presents worked only partially. She became more affectionate, more trusting—and that was it. So he went to his last resort. One morning, he ordered a horse to be saddled, dressed himself like a Circassian, armed himself, and went to her rooms.

"'Bela!' he said. 'You know how much I love you. I decided to carry you away, thinking that once you knew me, you would love me too. I was mistaken—farewell! You may be the mistress of everything I possess. If you want, you may return to your father—you are free. I am guilty before you and must punish myself. Farewell, I am going now. Where? How could I know? I may not manage to chase bullets or dodge the thrusts of swords for long: then think of me, and forgive me.' He turned away and reached his hand back toward her in a parting gesture. She didn't take the hand, and she said nothing. I could see through a crack as I stood behind the door and I felt such pity for her—such a deathly pallor had spread over that lovely little face!

"Not hearing a reply, Pechorin took a few steps toward the door; he was trembling—and shall I tell you? I think he was in such a state that he would have gone through with the business, though it all began in jest. That's what sort of person he was—unfathomable! He had barely touched the door when she jumped up, sobbed, and threw her arms around his neck. Can you believe it? Standing behind the door, I too started to weep, that's to say, you know, I didn't exactly weep, but just—what silliness!"

The staff captain went silent.

"Yes, I admit," he said after that, tugging at his mustache, "It started to bother me that no woman has ever loved me as much as that."

"And did their happiness last?" I asked.

"Yes, she confessed that from the first day she saw Pechorin, he often visited her dreams and that never has a man made such an impression on her. Yes, they were happy!"

"How boring!" I exclaimed without meaning to. I had really been expecting a tragic outcome, and suddenly my

hopes were unexpectedly dashed! "But, it can't be," I continued, "that the father didn't figure out that she was at the
fortress?"

"Well, it seems that he had his suspicions. A few days
later, we learned that the old man was killed. Here is how it
happened . . ."

My attention was awakened again.

"I should tell you that Kazbich imagined that Azamat had
stolen his horse with the consent of his father, at least that's
what I figure. So, one day, he waited on the road, at three
*verst*s from the *aul*. The old man was returning from a fruitless
search for his daughter. His retinue was some way behind, it
was twilight, and he was going along at an absentminded
pace. Suddenly Kazbich dived out of a bush like a cat, and,
with a thrust of his dagger, threw the prince to the ground,
took the reins—and was off. Some of the retinue had seen
the whole thing from a knoll and tore off in pursuit, only they
didn't catch him."

"He was compensating himself for the loss of his horse,
and taking his vengeance too," I said, to prompt an opinion
from my interlocutor.

"Of course, in their terms," said the staff captain, "he was
absolutely right."

I couldn't help but be struck by the Russian's ability to
adapt to the customs of the people among whom he finds
himself living. I don't know if this characteristic of mind deserves reprimand or praise, but it does prove his incredible
flexibility and the presence of that clear common sense, which
forgives evil where it seems unavoidable, or impossible to
destroy.

In the meantime, the tea had been drunk. Our horses, harnessed for some time now, were chilled to the bone in the
snow. The moon paled in the West and seemed prepared to
be plunged into her black clouds, hanging across the distant
peaks like the tatters of a ripped curtain. We emerged from
the *saklya*. Contrary to the predictions of my fellow traveler,
the weather had clarified and promised us a quiet morning.
Dances of stars wove themselves on the distant horizon into

marvelous patterns and one star after another was extinguished. A palish reflection from the east spread into the dark-violet vault of the sky, gradually illuminating the steep slopes of the mountain, covered in virgin snows. To the left and to the right somber, mysterious precipices grew black, and mists, twisting and winding like snakes, crawled along the wrinkles of the nearby rock-faces as though they were sensing the approaching day and were scared of it.

All was quiet on the earth and in the sky, like the heart of a person during the minute of morning prayer. But, occasionally a cool wind would spring up from the east, lifting the manes of the horses, which were coated in frost. We set off; five skinny nags hauled our carts with difficulty along the winding road up Gud Mountain. We walked on foot behind them, putting rocks behind the wheels when the horses ran out of strength. It looked as though the road led to the sky because as far as the eye could see, it kept ascending, and finally, became lost in the clouds, which had rested on the heights of Gud Mountain since the day before, like a kite awaiting its prey. The snow crunched under our feet; the air became so rare that it was painful to breathe; blood flooded into our heads every minute, and with it, some sort of gratifying feeling spread to every vein. I was so delighted to be so high above the world: it was a childlike feeling, I won't deny it, but withdrawing from the demands of society, and drawing near to nature, we become children without meaning to, and everything that has been acquired falls away from the soul—and it becomes as it once was, and probably will be once again. A person who has found himself wandering, like me, among desert mountains for a long, long time, and peering at their fantastical shapes, and who has greedily swallowed the life-giving air which pours into its gorges—that person, I'm certain, will understand my desire to relate, to tell, to paint these magical pictures. And so, at last, we gained the summit of Gud Mountain, stopped and looked around: there was a gray cloud suspended over it, and its cold breath threatened an approaching storm. But in the east, everything was so clear and golden, that we, that is the staff captain and I,

forgot about it completely . . . Yes, even the staff captain forgot: the simple people among us have hearts in which the
feeling of beauty, and the grandeur of nature, is stronger—a
hundredfold more vivid than in us, the rapturous storytellers
in words and on paper.

"I imagine you are used to these magnificent views . . ."
I said to him.

"And one can get used to the whistle of bullets too, that
is, used to hiding the involuntary throbbing of one's heart."

"I hear, on the contrary, that for some old soldiers such
music is even pleasing."

"Granted, it could be pleasing—but only because that same
heart is beating more strongly than usual.

"Look," he added, pointing to the east, "what country!"

Indeed, it is likely that I shall never again see the likes of
this panorama: the Koyshaursky Valley lay below us, inter-
sected by the Aragva River and another a small river, like two
silver threads. A light bluish mist was crawling along it, flee-
ing the warm rays of morning to the neighboring canyons.
On the left and the right, the hackles of the mountains, one
higher than the next, were criss-crossing and stretching along,
covered in snows, bushes. In the distance, there were similar
hills, where no two rock-faces were alike—and the snows
burned with a rosy luster, so uplifting, so bright, that it
seemed you could live here forever. The sun was just showing itself from behind the dark-blue mountains, which only
an accustomed eye could discern from the thunderclouds;
but there were blood-red streaks above the sun, to which my
comrade was paying particular attention.

"I told you," he exclaimed, "that there would be a lot of
weather today—we must hurry, otherwise, it will catch us on
the Krestovaya. Move along!" he cried to the cart drivers.

We put chains under the wheels as brakes to stop them
from rolling away, and we took the horses by their bridles
and started our descent. There was a crag on our right, and
such a precipice fell away to the left, that a whole village of
Ossetians living at its base looked like a swallow's nest. I shud-

dered at the thought that some ten times a year, in the deaf-
ness of night, some courier comes along this road, where two
carts can't pass at the same time, without once climbing off
his jolting carriage. One of our cart drivers was a Russian
muzhik[27] from Yaroslavl, the other was Ossetian. The Ossetian led his shaft-horse by the bridle, having taken every possible precaution, and unyoked the other horses beforehand.
But our carefree Russ[28] never once came down off his seat.
When I pointed out to him that he might take some care, not
least for the sake of my valise, after which I did not at all desire to clamber into this abyss, he replied to me, "Ah, sir! God
willing we'll do it no worse than anyone else has; we're not
the first." And he was right, we might not have made it, but
we did in fact make it, and if everyone discussed things more,
then they would convince themselves that life isn't worth the
constant worry . . .

But perhaps you want to know how the Bela story ends?
Firstly, I am not writing a novel, but travel notes: so it follows that I can't make the staff captain start recounting the
tale before he actually starts telling it to me. So, wait a while,
or, if you like, turn a few pages—only I don't advise you to
do that because the traverse across the Krestovaya Mountain
(or as the scholar Gamba calls it, the Mont St. Christophe)
is worthy of your interest.

So, we came down off Gud Mountain into the Chertova
Valley . . . now there's a romantic name! You immediately
imagine a nest of evil spirits in between the unassailable
crags—but not at all: the name of the Chertova Valley comes
from *cherta* (as in boundary) not *chert* (as in devil), because
apparently this was once the border of Georgia. This valley
was crammed with snowdrifts, rather vividly reminiscent
of Saratov, Tambov and other *dear little*[29] places of our
fatherland.

"That is Krestovaya!"[30] the staff captain said to me, when
we were traveling down into the Chertova Valley, pointing to
a mountain, covered in swaddling snow. A stone cross made
a black silhouette at its peak, and a road, just barely visible,

led past it, along which people travel when the road flanking
the hill is obstructed by snow. Our cart drivers relayed to us
that there hadn't yet been any avalanches, and, in consider-
ation of the horses, they led us around on the flanking road.
At the bend, we met about five men, Ossetians. They offered
us their services, and catching hold of our wheels, with one
cry, they took to dragging and supporting our carts. And to
be sure, the road was dangerous: on the right, heaps of snow
hung over our heads, ready, it seemed, to come away and fall
into the ravine at the first gust of wind. The narrow road
was partly covered in snow, which collapsed beneath your
feet in some parts, and in other places had turned into ice after the effects of sun-rays and night frosts, so that it was
with difficulty that we pushed our way through. The horses
fell from time to time; a deep fissure gaped to our left in
which a stream flowed downhill, sometimes hidden by an
icy crust, sometimes jumping with foam along the black
rocks. We barely managed to make our way around Krestovaya Mountain in two hours—two *verst*s in two hours! In the
meantime, the clouds had descended, pouring down hail and
snow. The wind, digging itself into the ravine, bellowed and
whistled like a Nightingale-Robber,[31] and soon the stone cross
was covered in mist, waves of which, one more dense and
more packed than the next, accumulated from the east . . .
Incidentally, a strange but universal legend exists about this
cross. It seems it was put here by Emperor Peter the First,
who traveled through the Caucasus. But first of all, Tsar Peter
had only been to Dagestan, and second, an engraving on the
cross in large letters says that the cross was put here under
the orders of General Yermolov in 1824 exactly. But the legend, ignoring the engraving, has taken root such that really,
you're not sure whom to believe, which is only added to by
the fact that we aren't used to believing engravings anyway.

We still had to descend about five *verst*s along the ice-
covered rock-face and muddy snows to reach Kobi station.
The horses were exhausted, and we were chilled to the bone.
The storm droned stronger and stronger, just like our native
northern storms—only this one's wild melodies were more

sad, more plaintive. "You're an exile too," I thought, "you cry for your wide, sweeping Steppe. There, you have room to unfurl your cold wings, but here it so stifled and cramped— you are like an eagle, who beats against the iron bars of his cage with a cry."

"No good!" said the staff captain. "See, nothing is visible here, only mist and snow, and you have to watch or we'll fall into an abyss or get lodged in a hole, and there, a little lower down, no doubt the Baidar River is running so high that you couldn't cross it. Such is Asia! Whether its people or its rivers, you can't count on anything in any way!"

With shouts and curses, the cart drivers thrashed the horses, which snorted, dug in their heels and wouldn't move from their places for anything on the earth, never mind the eloquence of the whips.

"Your Honor," one of them said finally, "it seems we won't get to Koba today. Will you not give the order, while you can, for us to turn left? You see, those are probably *saklyas* over there that blacken the landscape on the hillside. Travelers always stop there in bad weather; they're saying that they'll lead us through if you give them a little something for vodka," he added, pointing to the Ossetians.

"I know, old man, I know it without you telling me!" said the staff captain. "These rogues! They'll seize any chance in order to extract something for their vodka."

"You must admit, though," I said, "that things would be worse without them."

"Yes, that is so, that is so," he muttered, "but these cart drivers! They pick up the scent of advantage and take it when they can—and it's as if you wouldn't even find the road without them!"

Here, we turned to the left and somehow, after many obstacles, made it to the meager refuge, which consisted of two *saklyas,* connected by flagstones and cobblestones, and encircled by a wall of the same stone. We interrupted the hosts, who took us in cordially. I found out afterward that the government pays them and supports them under the condition that they take in travelers caught in storms.

"Things are improving!" I said, taking a seat at the fire. "Now you will tell me the rest of the story about Bela. I am sure that it didn't finish where you left it."

"And why are you so sure of that?" replied the staff captain, winking with a sly smile.

"From the fact that things are not settled. What started in an unusual way, should also end unusually."

"You've guessed it . . ."

"I'm glad."

"It is good that it gives you joy, but for me, really, it is sad to recollect it. She was a glorious girl, Bela! I became so used to her, by the end, it was as though she were a daughter, and she loved me. I have to tell you, that I don't have a family. Since the age of about twelve, I haven't heard a thing about my father or mother, and I didn't think to furnish myself with a wife earlier—and now, you know, it wouldn't be very becoming to do so. I was glad to have someone to spoil. She would sometimes sing us songs, or dance the *lezginka*[32] . . . and how she danced! I have seen our provincial gentlewomen, and once I was in Moscow at the Club of Nobility, about twenty years ago—but what of them! They were nothing in comparison! . . . Grigory Alexandrovich dressed her up like a doll, tended to her, pampered her, and she grew prettier, like a miracle. The suntan descended from her face and arms, and a pinkness got up into her cheeks . . . Oh, she was really something, happy, always playing tricks on me, the mischief-maker . . . God forgive her!"

"What happened when you told her about her father's death?"

"We hid it from her for a long time, while she was getting used to her situation. But when we told her, she cried for two days, and then forgot about it.

"About four months went by, and things couldn't have been better. Grigory Alexandrovich, I've already mentioned I think, loved hunting with a passion. He would sometimes have such an urge to go out after boar or wild goat—but during that time he wouldn't even step outside of the fortress ramparts. Then he started to seem distracted again; he paced his room, hands behind his back. And then once, without a word to anyone, he went off hunting, and was absent the whole morning. It happened again, and then it became more and more frequent . . . 'Not good,' I thought, 'it seems a black cat has run between them!'

"One morning I go in to see him when I see before my eyes: Bela sitting on the bed in a black silk *beshmet,* the poor pale thing was so sad that I took fright.

"'But where's Pechorin?' I asked.

"'Hunting.'

"'Did he leave today?' She was silent, as if it was hard for her to get it out.

"'No, yesterday,' she finally said, heavily exhaling.

"'Has something happened with him?'

"'I spent the whole day yesterday thinking and thinking,' she replied through tears, 'and came up with various misfortunes: it occurred to me that he had either been injured by a vicious wild boar, or that a Chechen had dragged him off into the hills . . . But now, it just seems to me that he doesn't love me.'

"'Really, my dear, you couldn't have thought up anything worse!'

"She started to cry and then, proudly raised her head, wiped away her tears, and continued:

"'If he doesn't love me, then who is preventing him from sending me home? I am not forcing him. But if it continues this way, then I'll go off myself: I am not his slave—I am the daughter of a prince!'

"I started to try to assure her.

"'Listen Bela, he can't sit here forever as if he were sewn to your skirts. He is a young man, and loves to chase wild things—he goes off, but he'll come back. And if you're going to pine, then he'll soon tire of it.'

"'True, true!' she replied. "I'll be cheerful.'

"And with a loud laugh, she took up her tambourine, started to sing, dance, and bounce around me. Only this didn't last long, and again she fell down on the bed and covered her face with her hands.

"What was I to do with her? I have never interacted much with women, you know. I was thinking and thinking about what might comfort her and couldn't think of a thing. We were both silent for a time . . . A very unpleasant situation!

"Finally I said to her: 'Why don't we go for a walk along the ramparts? The weather is glorious!' This was September. And really, the day was marvelous, bright and it wasn't hot. All the mountains were visible, as if laid out on a platter. We went and walked along the fortress ramparts, back and forth, in silence. Finally she sat on some grass, and I sat next to her. But really, it's funny to look back and think about how I ran around after her, like some sort of nanny.

"Our fortress stood at a high point, and the view from the ramparts was excellent. On one side, there was a wide glade, pitted with several gullies, finishing at a forest that stretched to the peak of the mountain. Here and there, *auls* were sending up smoke, herds were ranging. A rivulet ran on the other side, flanked by the thick shrubbery, which covered the stony ridges connecting to the central chain of the Caucasus. We sat on the corner of a bastion, so we could see everything on either side. And then I saw: someone emerging from the forest on a gray horse, getting closer and closer, and finally stopping on the other side of the stream, about a hundred *sazhens*[33] from us, and twirling his horse, like a madman. What an extraordinary thing!

"'Look there, Bela,' I said, 'you have young eyes, who is this *dzhigit*—and who is he here to entertain?'

"She looked over and cried out, 'It's Kazbich!'

"'Ach, that scamp! What—has he come to laugh at us?' I'm peering down and she's right, it's Kazbich: that's his swarthy snout, ragged and dirty, as always.

"'That's my father's horse,' said Bela, grabbing my hand. She was shaking like a leaf and her eyes were sparkling. 'Aha!' I thought, 'that roguish blood hasn't quieted down in you either, my darling!'

"'Come over here,' I said to the sentry. 'Train your rifle, and help this clever man off his horse—and you'll get a silver ruble for it!'

"'Yes, Your Honor. But he isn't standing still!'

"'Make him move!' I said, laughing . . .

"'Hello there, kind sir!' shouted the sentry, waving at him. 'Slow down, why are you twirling like a spinning top?'

"Kazbich actually stopped and started to listen attentively—he probably thought that someone was initiating negotiations with him—not at all!

"My grenadier took aim . . . Batz! . . . Missed. As soon as the gunpowder flared at the barrel, Kazbich nudged his horse and it leapt to the side. He came up a little in his stirrups and cried something in his own language, threatening us with his whip—and that was the last we saw of him.

"'Shame on you!' I said to the sentry.

"'Your Honor! He's gone off to die,' he replied. 'Those damned people don't die instantly.'

"A quarter of an hour later, Pechorin returned from hunting. Bela threw herself around his neck, without complaint, without any reproach for his long absence . . .

"But even I was getting angry with him. 'For pity's sake,' I said, 'just here, a moment ago, Kazbich was by the stream and we fired at him. It's been a while since you've come across him, hasn't it? These mountain-dwelling people are vindictive. Do you think he has guessed that you had a part in helping Azamat? I'll wager that he recognized Bela just now. And I know that about a year ago, he liked her tremendously—he told me so himself—and if he had figured out how to collect a decent amount of bride-money, then he'd probably have sought a marriage with her . . .'

"Pechorin then fell to thinking. 'Yes,' he replied, 'we must be more careful . . . Bela, from today you must not walk on the fortress ramparts.'

"In the evening, I had a long, elucidating discussion with him. I was vexed that he had so changed toward the poor girl. Apart from the fact that he would spend half the day hunting, his treatment of her had turned cold, he rarely caressed her, and she had noticeably started to wither, her little face was drawn, and her big eyes had lost their luster.

"Sometimes you would ask her:

" 'Why such a big sigh Bela? Are you sad?'

" 'No!'

" 'Is there something you would like?'

" 'No!'

" 'Do you miss your kin?'

" 'I don't have kin.'

"Sometimes you would get nothing more than 'yes' or 'no' out of her for whole days.

"So I told him as much.

" 'Listen, Maxim Maximych,' he replied. 'I have an unfortunate character—whether it is how I was brought up, or whether God created me this way, I don't know. I only know that if I am the cause of unhappiness in others, then I am no less unhappy myself. In my early youth, from the moment I left the care of my parents, I began furiously enjoying all the many pleasures you can obtain for money, and then, it seems, these pleasures became loathsome to me. Then I set forth into the wide world, and soon I'd had enough of society too. I fell in love with society beauties and was loved by them too—but their love only inflamed my imagination and pride, leaving my heart empty . . . I started to read, to study—but academics also bored me. I realized that neither glory nor happiness depends on them, because the happiest people are the ignorant. Glory comes from good fortune, and to attain it, you must merely be cunning. And then everything became tedious . . . Soon after, they transferred me to the Caucasus: this was the happiest time of my life. I hoped that boredom didn't exist under Chechen bullets, but it was in vain—within a month I was so used to their whirring and to the nearness of death, that really, I paid more attention to the mosquitoes. And I was more bored than before, because I had lost what was nearly my last hope. When I saw Bela in my home, when for the first time I held her on my knees, I kissed her black curls, like a fool, I thought that she was an angel, sent to me by compassionate Fate . . . I was again mistaken. The love of a savage girl is not much better than the love of a noblewoman. The ignorance and simple-heartedness of the one becomes as tiresome as the coquettishness of the other. If you like, I still love her, I am grateful to her for several sufficiently sweet minutes. I would give my life for her, only I am bored in her company . . . Whether I'm a fool or a scoundrel, I don't know. But one thing is sure—that I am as worthy of pity, maybe even more so, as she is. The soul inside me is corrupted by the world, my imagination is restless, my heart is insatiable. Nothing is ever enough. I have become as used to sorrow as I am to delight, and my life becomes more empty from one day to the next. There is only one remedy left for me: travel. As soon as I can, I will set off—only not to Europe, God forbid! I'll go to America, to Arabia, to India— maybe I'll perish somewhere along the way! At least, I am certain, that this final solace will not be exhausted too quickly, with the help of storms and bad roads.'

"He spoke like this for a long time, and his words engraved themselves on my memory because it was the first time I had heard such things from a twenty-five-year-old, and, God willing, it will be the last . . . How extraordinary!

"So tell me," the staff captain continued, addressing himself to me, "from the sound of things, you have been in the capital recently—surely the youth there are not all like that?"

I answered that there are many people who speak in the same way; that there are, probably, some that are telling the truth; however, disillusionment, like every fashion, having begun at the highest social strata, had descended to the lower strata, who were now wearing it out, and that now, those who are most bored of all try to hide this misfortune as though it were a vice. The staff captain didn't understand these nuances, shook his head, and smiled slyly.

"And it was the French, no doubt, who brought in this fashion of boredom?"

"No, the English."

"Aha, that's it!" he replied. "Indeed, they have always been inveterate drunks!"

I couldn't help remembering one Muscovite lady, who had assured me that Byron had been nothing more than a drunk. But the staff captain's observation was more pardonable: in order to restrain himself from wine, he, of course, was trying to persuade himself that all the misfortunes of the world have their origins in drink.

Meanwhile, he continued his story in this way:

"Kazbich didn't appear again. Only, and I don't know why, I couldn't get the thought out of my head that it was not for nothing that he had come, and that he was preparing himself for something nefarious.

"One day, Pechorin had tried to persuade me to go boar-hunting with him. I refused at length. Wild boar was no marvel to me! But, he managed to drag me off with him anyway. We took about five soldiers and set off early in the morning. Until ten o'clock we darted about the rushes and forest without seeing one beast.

"'Ho! Shouldn't we go back?' I said. 'What is there to aim at? It's clear that it's turned out to be an unlucky day!' But Grigory Alexandrovich did not want to turn back without some sort of quarry, never mind the intense heat and exhaustion . . . that's the kind of person he was—as soon as something occurs to him, he has to have it. He must have been spoiled by his mama as a child . . . Finally, at midday, we tracked down a damned boar. Paff! Paff! . . . No luck. It fled into the rushes. That's the sort of unlucky day it was! . . . Then we paused to catch our breath for a moment, and set off home.

"We rode side by side, saying nothing, with loose reins, and we were right near the fortress—only bushes were hiding it from view. Suddenly a shot was fired . . . and we looked at each other. We were seized by the same suspicion . . . We galloped headlong toward the shot, and saw that soldiers had gathered in a bunch on the ramparts and were pointing to a field. And there, flying along, was a horseman carrying something white in his saddle. Grigory Alexandrovich gave out a cry worthy of a Chechen, pulled his rifle from its case and was off. I followed.

"Fortunately, due to our unsuccessful hunting efforts, our horses were not worn out, they strained under our saddles, and with each moment we were closer and closer . . . And at last, I recognized Kazbich, though I couldn't make out what it was that he was holding in front of him. I drew up to Pechorin and yelled to him: 'It's Kazbich!' And he looked at me, nodded, and struck his horse with his whip.

"At last we were within a rifle shot's distance of him. Whether it was that Kazbich's horse was exhausted, or that it was a worse horse than ours, much as he tried, it wasn't making much progress. I imagine at that moment Kazbich was harking back to his Karagyoz . . .

"As I watched, Pechorin took aim with his rifle at full gallop . . . 'Don't shoot!' I yelled to him. 'Hold your fire! We'll catch up with him!' But—young men! Forever flaring up when they shouldn't . . . A shot rang out, and the bullet broke the horse's back leg. It sprang along another ten times or so, compelled by the heat of the moment, then stumbled and fell to its knees. Kazbich leapt off, and then we saw that he was holding a woman covered in a *yashmak* in his arms . . . It was Bela . . . Poor Bela! He then shouted something in his tongue and raised his dagger over her . . . There wasn't a moment to waste. I took a shot in turn, a random shot. It looked as though the bullet had hit him in the shoulder be-cause his arm suddenly fell . . . But when the smoke had dis-persed, the horse lay wounded on the ground, and Bela next to it. And Kazbich, having thrown his rifle into the bushes, was clambering up the cliff like a cat. I would have liked to pick him off, but I didn't have a ready cartridge! We jumped off our horses and rushed to Bela. The poor thing, she was lying there, unmoving, and blood was pouring in streams from her wound. That scoundrel—he could have at least struck her in the heart and ended it all with one blow, but to stick her in the back . . . the most treacherous of attacks! She wasn't conscious. We tore up the *yashmak* and bandaged the wound as tightly as we could. Pechorin kissed her cold lips, but to no avail—nothing could bring her to her senses.

"Pechorin mounted his horse. I lifted her from the ground and somehow installed her in his saddle. He embraced her with his arm, and we went back to the fortress. After several minutes of silence, Grigory Alexandrovich said to me, 'Listen, Maxim Maximych, we won't get her back alive like this.'

" 'Right!' I said. We gave our horses their heads, and rode at full tilt. A crowd of people awaited us at the gates of the fortress. Carefully we transferred the wounded girl to Pechorin's quarters and sent for the doctor. Though he was drunk, he made it; he inspected her wound and announced that she wouldn't live more than a day—but he was mistaken . . ."

"Did she get better?" I asked the staff captain, grabbing his arm, unable to help myself from feeling glad.

"No," he replied, "the doctor was mistaken in that she lasted two more days."

"But explain to me—how did Kazbich manage to kidnap her?"

"Here's how: in spite of Pechorin's rules, she left the fortress and went down to the stream. It was, you see, very hot that day. She was sitting on a rock and lowered her feet into the water. Then Kazbich crept up and grabbed her, covered her mouth, and dragged her into the bushes, where he jumped on his horse and he was off! In the meantime she managed to let out a cry, the sentry was alerted, and he fired a shot, which missed, and that's when we appeared."

"But why did Kazbich want to take her?"

"For pity's sake! These Circassians are notoriously thieving folk. If anything is lying around, they can't help but pinch it. Even if they don't need it, they'll steal it anyway . . . but they must be forgiven for that! Besides, he had liked her for a long time."

"And Bela died?"

"She died. But she suffered for a long time, and we suffered very much with her. At about ten o'clock in the evening she came to. We were sitting at her bedside and as soon as she opened her eyes, she started asking for Pechorin.

" 'I'm here, beside you, my *djanechka*,' he replied (our word for this is 'sweetheart'), taking her hand. 'I am dying!' she said. We started comforting her, saying that the doctor had promised to cure her without fail. She shook her head and turned toward the wall: she didn't want to die!

"That night she started to become delirious. Her head was burning, the trembling of a fever ran up and down her body.

She was uttering disconnected phrases about her father, her brother. She wanted to go to the mountains, to go home . . . Then she also started speaking about Pechorin, calling him various affectionate things or reproaching him for ceasing to love his *djanechka* . . .

"He listened to her without saying anything, his head lowered into his hands. But I never once noticed a tear on his lashes. Indeed, he either couldn't cry or he was containing himself—I don't know. Personally, I have never laid eyes on anything more pitiable.

"The delirium lifted toward morning. For an hour, she lay there motionless and pale, with such feebleness that it was barely possible to see her breathing. Then she seemed better, and she started talking—but what do you think she was on about? . . . This kind of thing only occurs to the dying! She had started lamenting the fact that she wasn't a Christian, and that in the other world, her soul wouldn't meet Pechorin's, and that some other woman would become his companion in heaven. I had an idea to christen her before she died and I suggested it to her. She looked at me with indecision and couldn't utter anything for a long while. Eventually, she responded saying she would die of the same faith with which she was born. A whole day passed in this way. How she changed over the course of that day! Her pale cheeks sank, her eyes grew larger and larger, her lips burned. She felt an inner heat, as though there was a piece of burning-hot iron in her breast.

"The next night fell; we didn't close our eyes, didn't leave her bedside. She was suffering terribly, moaning, and when the pain subsided, she would try to convince Grigory Alexandrovich that she was better, persuading him to get some sleep, she kissed his hand, she wouldn't release it from her own. Before morning she began to feel the anguish of death, she started to toss around, dislodged her bandage, and she bled again. When they dressed the wound, she was calm for a minute and started asking Pechorin if he would kiss her. He got onto his knees by the bed, lifted her head a little from the pillow, and pressed his lips to her ever-colder lips. She threw her shaking arms tightly around his neck as though with this kiss she wanted to convey her soul to him . . . But she did well to die! What would have become of her if Grigory Alexandrovich had abandoned her? It would have happened sooner or later . . .

"The first half of the next day she was quiet, un-talking and obedient, as the doctor tortured her with poultices and mixtures.

" 'For pity's sake!' I said to him. 'You said yourself that she would die for certain, so why all these medical preparations?'

" 'It's still better than nothing, Maxim Maximych,' he responded, 'for the sake of a peaceful conscience.' A peaceful conscience!

"After midday, she started to be tormented by thirst. We opened the window, but it was hotter in the courtyard than in her room. We put pieces of ice by her bed but nothing was helping. I knew that this was an unbearable thirst—a sign of the approaching end—and told this to Pechorin. 'Water! Water!' she said with a hoarse voice, rising up slightly in her bed.

"He became as white as a sheet, grabbed a glass, poured water into it and gave it to her. I covered my eyes with my hands and started to recite a prayer, I don't remember which . . . Yes, my dear sir, I have often seen people dying in hospitals and on battlefields—but it didn't compare—didn't compare! . . . And what's more, I should confess, that there's something that particularly saddens me: she didn't once think of me before her death. And, it seems, I loved her like a father . . . God forgive her! . . . But, in actuality, it must be said: who am I that she should remember me before her death?

"As soon as she had taken a drink of water, she felt a certain ease, and after three minutes she perished. We put a mirror up to her lips—it was clear! . . . I led Pechorin straight out of the room, and we went to the fortress ramparts. For a long time we walked back and forth along the ramparts side by side, without saying a word, our hands clasped behind our backs. His face expressed nothing in particular and

I became vexed. In his place I would have died of grief. Eventually, he sat on the ground, in the shade, and started scratching something in the sand with a stick. I wanted to comfort him, and started to say something, mostly out of a sense of decency, you know. And he raised his head and burst out laughing . . . a chill ran along my skin with that laughter . . . I went off to order the coffin.

"I admit that I was occupying myself with this task partly in order to distract myself. I had a piece of *thermalam*,[34] with which I lined her coffin, and I decorated it with the Circassian silver galloon, which Grigory Alexandrovich had bought for her earlier anyway.

"The next day, in the early morning, we buried her behind the fortress, by the stream, near the place where last she had sat. White acacia and elders have now spread around her grave. I wanted to mount a cross, but, you know, it wouldn't be right: after all, she wasn't a Christian . . ."

"And what happened to Pechorin?" I asked.

"Pechorin was unwell for a long while, he wasted away, poor fellow, but we never spoke of Bela again. I saw that it would have been unpleasant for him—so why mention it? About three months later he was appointed to the E—— regiment and he left for Georgia. We haven't seen each other since then . . . Yes, I seem to remember someone telling me not long ago that he had returned to Russia, but it wasn't in corps orders. But then, news is always late in arriving to the likes of us."

Then he launched into a long dissertation about how unpleasant it is to receive news a year after the fact—probably in an effort to dampen his sad memories.

I didn't interrupt him, but I didn't listen either.

After an hour, an opportunity to continue our journey arose. The blizzard had abated, the sky had cleared, and we set off. On the road, I couldn't help but start a conversation about Bela and Pechorin again.

"Did you ever hear what happened to Kazbich?" I asked.

"To Kazbich? I really don't know . . . I heard that there is some Kazbich in the right flank of the *Shapsugs,* a daring fellow, who rides around at a slow pace under our fire, and very courteously takes a bow when a bullet buzzes near him—but it's unlikely that it's the same man!"

In Kobi I parted ways with Maxim Maximych. I went on, traveling post, and he was unable to follow me since his load was heavy. We didn't have a hope of ever meeting again, but nonetheless we did. And if you like, I'll tell you about it—but that's another story . . . Won't you agree, however, that Maxim Maximych is a man worthy of respect? . . . If you agree, then I will have been rewarded for my story, overlong though it may have been.

II
MAXIM MAXIMYCH

Having parted ways with Maxim Maximych, I galloped quickly through the Terek Gorge and the Daryal, stopped for dinner at Kazbek, had tea at Lars, and made it to Vladikavkaz for supper. I will spare you from descriptions of the mountains, from exclamations that express nothing, from pictures that depict nothing—especially for those of you who have not been there—and from those statistical notes that nobody can bear to read.

I stopped at the inn where travelers always stop but where, nonetheless, there is no one of whom to request a roast pheasant or some cabbage soup, for the three veteran soldiers in charge of it are so stupid or so drunk that no sense can be got out of them.

I was informed that I would have to endure another three days here since the *Opportunity* from Ekaterinograd hadn't yet arrived, and hence could not set off back again. What opportunity! . . . But a bad pun isn't much comfort to a Russian man, and for amusement's sake, I struck on the idea of writing down Maxim Maximych's tale about Bela, not imagining that this would be the first link in a long chain of stories. How insignificant happenings sometimes have cruel consequences! . . . Perhaps you don't know what the *Opportunity* is? It is a convoy, consisting of a half company of infantry and a cannon, which escorts transports through the Kabarde, from Vladikavkaz to Ekaterinograd.

The first day I spent there was very boring. The next day a cart rolled into the courtyard in the early morning . . .

Ah! Maxim Maximych! . . . We greeted each other like old friends. I invited him to stay in my quarters. He didn't stand on ceremony, and he even clapped me on the shoulder and twisted his mouth into the semblance of a smile. What an eccentric!

Maxim Maximych possessed a deep knowledge of the culinary arts: he roasted a pheasant amazingly well, and successfully added a cucumber brine to it, and I must admit that without him there would have only been dry food left to me. A bottle of Kakhetian wine helped us to forget the modest number of dishes, which amounted to all of one, and having smoked a pipe, we settled in—I sat by the window and he by the heated stove, because the day had been damp and cold. We were silent. What was there to talk about? . . . He had already told me everything that was of interest about himself, and I had nothing to tell. I looked through the window. A multitude of low dwellings twinkled among the trees, scattered along the banks of the Terek River, which runs more and more widely here; and in the distance a toothy wall of mountains shined blue, and from behind them the peak of Mount Kazbek emerged in its white cardinal's hat. I said farewell to them in my thoughts and I was sorry to do so . . .

We sat like that for a long time. The sun had hidden itself behind the cold peaks, and a whitish mist had begun to disperse in the valley, when the sound of a harness bell and the shouts of cart drivers resounded in the street. Several carts of dirty-looking Armenians drove into the courtyard of the inn; an empty carriage arrived behind them, with an easy gait, a comfortable construction and dandified appearance—all of which gave it some sort of stamp of foreignness. A man with a large mustache walked behind it, wearing a *dolman*,[1] looking rather well-dressed for a lackey. But it was impossible to mistake his position, seeing the rakish manner with which he shook the ash from his pipe and shouted at the coachman. He was clearly the spoiled servant of a lazy master—a sort of Russian *Figaro*.

"Tell me, my good man," I cried to him from the window, "is this the *Opportunity* that has arrived?"

He looked at me impertinently, adjusted his tie and turned around. There was an Armenian walking next to him, smiling, who replied for him that the *Opportunity* had indeed arrived and tomorrow morning it would set off back again.

"Thank God!" said Maxim Maximych, walking up to the window at that moment. "What a marvelous carriage!" he added. "There's probably some official heading to an inquiry in Tiflis. But he obviously doesn't know our hills! No, he can't be serious, the good man—these hills aren't kind—they'll give a good jolting even to an English carriage!"

"But who do you think he is? Let's go and find out . . ." We went out into the corridor. At the end of the corridor, the door to a side room was open. The lackey and the coachman were dragging valises inside.

"Listen, my friend," the staff captain asked him, "whose is this marvelous carriage, eh? It's an excellent carriage!"

The lackey, not turning around, mumbled something to himself as he unfastened the valise. Maxim Maximych became angry; he touched the rude man on the shoulder and said:

"I'm talking to you, good man."

"Whose carriage? . . . It's my master's . . ."

"And who is your master?"

"Pechorin . . ."

"Really? Really? Pechorin? . . . Oh good God! . . . Did he perhaps once serve in the Caucasus?" exclaimed Maxim Maximych, tugging at my sleeve. Joy was sparkling in his eyes.

"Yes, he did, I'd guess—but I haven't been with him for long."

"Well there you go! There it is! Grigory Alexandrovich? . . . That's his name, right? . . . Your master and I were friends," he added, slapping the lackey fraternally on the shoulder so hard that it caused the man to stagger . . .

"If you please, sir, you are getting in my way," said the man, frowning.

"Well, look at that! . . . Do you understand? Your master and I were once the best of friends, we lived together . . . So, where is the man himself?"

The servant declared that Pechorin had stopped to dine and spend the night with Colonel N——.

"Won't he drop by here this evening?" said Maxim Maximych. "Or will you, good man, be going to him for anything? . . . If you are, will you tell him that Maxim Maximych is here. Tell him that. He'll understand . . . I'll give you eighty *kopeck*s for your vodka."

The lackey assumed a contemptuous demeanor hearing such a modest pledge, but assured Maxim Maximych that he would fulfill his instructions.

"He'll come running, you'll see!" Maxim Maximych told me with a triumphant air, "I'll go to the gate and wait for him . . . Eh! It's a shame that I'm not acquainted with N—— . . ."

Maxim Maximych sat in front of the gate on a bench, and I went back to my room. I'll admit I also awaited the appearance of this Pechorin with a certain amount of impatience, though from the staff captain's tale I had formed an opinion of him that wasn't very favorable. But several features of his character seemed remarkable to me. After an hour, one of the veterans brought a boiling samovar and a teapot.

"Maxim Maximych, would you like some tea?" I called to him through the window.

"I thank you, but I don't really want any."

"Come now, have some! Look here, it's late already, and cold."

"No, it's fine, thank you."

"As you like!"

I started drinking my tea alone, and about ten minutes later my old friend came in.

"Indeed, you're right—it's a good idea to have some tea. I just kept waiting . . . his man went to get him a while ago, and it seems something has kept them."

He quickly drank down a teacup, refused a second and went out again to the gate in some agitation. Clearly the old man was distressed at Pechorin's negligence, not least because he had recently told me about his friendship with Pechorin, and an hour or so ago he had been sure that Pechorin would come running at the mention of his name.

It was already late and dark when I opened the window again and started calling to Maxim Maximych, saying that it was time to retire. He muttered something between his teeth. I repeated my call and he didn't reply.

I lay on the divan, wrapped in a greatcoat, and soon dozed off, leaving a candle on the stove-bench. And I would have slept soundly if it had not been for Maxim Maximych, who entered the room when it was already very late and awakened me. He threw his pipe on the table, and started to walk up and down the room, throwing logs into the stove, and finally he lay down, but coughed for a long time, spat a few times, tossed around . . .

"Have you got fleas perhaps?" I asked.

"Yes, it's fleas," he replied, exhaling heavily.

I woke early the next morning. But Maxim Maximych had anticipated me. I found him by the gate, sitting on the bench.

"I have to go to the commandant," he said, "so please, if Pechorin arrives, send someone to get me . . ."

I promised. He ran off . . . as though his limbs had been newly endowed with youthful energy and flexibility.

The morning was cooler, but beautiful. Golden clouds towered over the hills: another row of mountains, made of air. A wide square extended in front of the gate, beyond which a bazaar seethed with people, since it was Sunday. Barefoot Ossetian boys carrying sacks of honeycombs circled around me again and again. I chased them off. I didn't want anything from them, and I was starting to share the anxieties of the good staff captain.

Not ten minutes had passed before the person we had been waiting for appeared at one end of the square. He was walking with Colonel N——, who led him to the inn, said farewell and turned back to his fort. I immediately sent one of the veterans to get Maxim Maximych.

Pechorin's lackey came out to meet his master and reported that they were harnessing the horses. He then gave him a box of cigars and, having received several orders, went off to take care of things. Pechorin lit a cigar, yawned a couple of times and sat on the bench on the other side of the gate. Now, I must paint a portrait of him for you.

He was of medium height and well-proportioned; his slim waist and broad shoulders indicated a strong physique, capable of withstanding all the hardships of a life wandering through varying climes, and which was neither defeated by the debauchery of life in the capital, nor by storms of the soul. His dusty velvet frock coat, fastened only by its two lowest buttons, allowed a view of his blindingly white linen, indicating the habits of a proper gentleman. His soiled gloves appeared to have been specially sewn for his small aristocratic hands, and when he took off one glove, I was surprised at the thinness of his pale fingers. His gait was careless and lazy, but I noticed that he didn't swing his arms—a clear signal of a certain secretiveness of character. However, these are my own comments, based on my own observations, and I absolutely do not want to make you take them on blind faith. When he lowered himself onto the bench, his straight figure bent as though there wasn't a bone in his back. The position of his body expressed a nervous feebleness. He sat the way Balzac's thirty-year-old coquette[2] would sit, on a chair stuffed with down, after an exhausting ball. From an initial glance at him, I wouldn't have given him more than twenty-three years in age, but later, I would be prepared to give him thirty. There was something childlike in his smile. His skin had a sort of feminine delicacy to it; he had blond hair, wavy in nature, which outlined his pale, noble brow so picturesquely— a brow, which, upon long observation, revealed traces of wrinkles, criss-crossing each other, probably showing themselves much more distinctly in moments of anger or agitation of the soul. However blond his hair was, his whiskers and eyebrows were black—the mark of breeding in a person, as is the black mane and tail of a white horse. To complete the portrait, I will tell you that he had a slightly upturned nose, blindingly white teeth, and brown eyes. About his eyes, I must say a few more words.

First of all, they didn't laugh when he laughed! Have you never noticed such an oddity in certain people? . . . This is a sign either of an evil disposition, or of deep and perpetual sorrow. From under half-lowered eyelashes, they shone with a sort of phosphorescent gleam (if you can call it that). It wasn't the reflection of his soul's fire or his imagination's playfulness, but it was a glint similar to the glint of smooth steel: dazzling but cold. His gaze was fleeting but piercing and weighted, leaving you with the unpleasant impression that you have been asked an immodest question. And it might have seemed impertinent, had he not been so indifferent and calm. All these thoughts came to mind perhaps because I knew several details of his life, and maybe to someone else's eyes he would produce a completely differing impression. But since you haven't heard about him from anyone else but me, then you will have to suffice yourselves with this depiction. I will tell you, in conclusion, that he was altogether not at all bad-looking and had one of those original physiognomies, which is especially appealing to society ladies.

The horses were already harnessed; a small bell rang from time to time under the shaft-bow, and the lackey had already twice approached Pechorin with the report that everything was ready, and Maxim Maximych still hadn't appeared. Fortunately, Pechorin was immersed in reverie, looking over at the blue teeth of the Caucasus, and it seems he was not hurrying in the least to take to the road. I walked up to him.

"If you don't mind waiting a little longer," I said, "then you will have the pleasure of encountering an old friend . . ."

"Yes, of course!" he quickly replied, "I was told yesterday—where is he after all?"

I turned toward the square and saw Maxim Maximych running with all his might . . . A few minutes later, he was by our side. He could barely breathe. Sweat rolled in torrents down his face. Wet wisps of gray hair, which had broken

loose from under his hat, were sticking to his forehead. His
knees were shaking . . . He wanted to throw his arms around
Pechorin's neck, but the latter was rather cold, albeit giving
a friendly smile, and extended his hand to him. The staff captain was stopped in his tracks, but soon greedily grasped the
hand with both his hands. He still couldn't speak.

"How glad I am, dear Maxim Maximych! Well, how are
you, sir?" said Pechorin.

"And you? And you . . . sir?" muttered the old man with
tears in his eyes, "how many years it's been . . . how many
days . . . where are you going?"

"I am going to Persia, and beyond . . ."

"But not at this moment? . . . Come now, wait, my very
dear friend! . . . Don't tell me we're to part now? . . . How
long it has been since we last saw each other . . ."

"I must go, Maxim Maximych," was the answer.

"Good God! Good God! Where are you going in such a
rush? . . . I have so many things I'd like to tell you . . . so
much to find out . . . But tell me—have you retired? . . . How
are things? . . . What have you been doing?"

"Tedium!" Pechorin replied, smiling.

"And do you remember our days at the fortress? . . .
Glorious countryside for hunting! . . . You were an ardent
hunter . . . and Bela?"

Pechorin went slightly pale, and turned away . . .

"Yes, I remember!" he said, forcing a yawn almost
immediately . . .

Maxim Maximych started to prevail upon him to remain
for another couple of hours.

"We will have a splendid dinner," he said, "I have two
pheasants, and the Kakhetian wine here is excellent . . . well,
it goes without saying that it's not the same as the one you
find in Georgia, but it's a fine variety . . . We can talk . . . You
can tell me about your life in Petersburg . . . Eh?"

"Really, I have nothing to tell, my dear Maxim
Maximych . . . And farewell, it's time I leave . . . I'm in a
hurry . . . Thank you for not having forgotten . . ." he added,
taking him by the hand.

The old man crossed his brows . . . He was sad and angry, though he tried to hide it.

"Forgotten!" he muttered, "I haven't forgotten a thing . . . Well, godspeed . . . but this is not how I imagined our reunion . . ."

"Come, come!" said Pechorin, embracing him amiably, "have I changed so much? . . . What's to be done? . . . To each his own path . . . May we meet again—God willing . . . !" And having said that, he seated himself in his carriage as the coachman began to gather up the reins.

"Wait! Wait" cried Maxim Maximych suddenly, grabbing at the doors of the carriage, "I completely forgot . . . I have, in my possession, your papers, Grigory Alexandrovich . . . I carry them with me . . . thinking I would find you in Georgia, and here God has granted us a meeting . . . What shall I do with them?"

"Whatever you like!" responded Pechorin, "Farewell . . ."

"So, you're off to Persia . . . And when will you return?" Maxim Maximych cried in pursuit.

The carriage was already far off, but Pechorin made a gesture with his hand that could be translated as saying: It's unlikely! What for, anyway?

The sounds of the small bells and the clattering of the wheels on the stony road had long fallen silent while the poor old man still stood in place, deep in thought.

"Yes," he said at last, attempting to adopt an indifferent air, though the tears of vexation occasionally glittered on his eyelashes, "of course, we were friends—but, then, what are friends in this day and age? Who am I to him? I am not rich, not a person of rank, yes, and I don't match him in age . . . Just look at what a dandy he has made of himself, since he visited Petersburg again . . . And what a carriage! . . . How much luggage! . . . And such a proud lackey!"

These words were enunciated with an ironic smile.

"So tell me," he continued, addressing himself to me. "What do you think of all this? . . . What kind of demon is driving him to Persia? . . . Droll, oh Lord, it's droll . . . Yes, I always knew that he was a fickle friend, on whom you

couldn't depend . . . And, really, it's a shame, he shall come
to a bad end . . . there's no escaping it! . . . I always said that
those who forget their old friends are no good!"

At that he turned around, in order to hide his emotion,
and went off to pace in the courtyard by his cart, as though
he was inspecting the wheels, his eyes filling with tears over
and over again.

"Maxim Maximych," I said, walking up to him, "and
what are these papers that Pechorin has left with you?"

"God knows! Notes of some kind . . ."

"What will you do with them?"

"What? I'll order cartridges to be made of them."

"You'd do better to give them to me."

He looked at me with surprise, muttered something through
his teeth and started to rummage in a valise. He then pulled
out a book of diaries and threw it with contempt onto the
ground. Then there was a second, a third and a tenth, all
given the same treatment. There was something puerile in
his vexation. It incited amusement, but my compassion too . . .

"That's the lot," he said, "I congratulate you on your
find . . ."

"And may I do what I like with them?"

"Publish them in the newspapers if you like. What business is it of mine?! . . . Who am I to him—some kind of
friend, a relative? . . . True, we lived under one roof for a
long while . . . But there's many a person I have shared roofs
with!"

I grabbed the papers and quickly took them away, fearing
that the staff captain might regret it. Soon after that we were
told that the *Opportunity* would set off an hour later. I ordered the horses harnessed. The staff captain came into my
room just as I had put on my hat. He, it seemed, was not getting ready for the departure. He had a tense and cold look
to him.

"And you, Maxim Maximych, are you not coming?"

"No, sir."

"And why not?"

"Well, I still haven't seen the commandant, and I need to hand over some State property . . ."

"But weren't you just with him?"

"I was, of course," he said, stumbling over his words, "he wasn't at home . . . and I didn't wait."

I understood him. The poor old man, for perhaps the first time since his birth, had abandoned official business for personal necessity—in the parlance of paper-pushing people—and look how he was rewarded!

"It's a real pity," I said to him, "a real pity, Maxim Maximych, that we must part sooner than originally planned."

"What do you need with the likes of an ill-educated old man running behind you! You young folk are fashionable and pompous: it's all right when you're here under Circassian bullet-fire . . . but meet you later, and you're too ashamed to even hold out your hand to a person like me."

"I don't deserve these reproaches, Maxim Maximych."

"No, I was just talking by the by, as it were; but, anyway, I wish you every happiness and pleasant travels."

We said our farewells with a certain dryness. The kind Maxim Maximych had turned into a stubborn, quarrelsome staff captain! And why? Because Pechorin, in his distraction or for some other reason, shook his hand when the staff captain would have liked to throw his arms around Pechorin's neck! It is sad to see a youth lose his best hopes and aspirations, when the pink *chiffon* in front of him—through which he had seen the matters and feelings of humankind—is pulled aside. However, there is at least the hope that they will exchange their old misgivings for new ones, which are no less temporary yet no less sweet . . . But what can a man of Maxim Maximych's years replace them with? The heart will harden without wishing to, and the soul will take cover . . .

I departed alone.

PECHORIN'S DIARIES

Foreword

I learned not long ago that Pechorin had died upon returning from Persia. This news made me very glad: it gave me the right to publish these notes, and I took the opportunity to put my name on someone else's work. God grant that readers won't punish me for this innocent forgery.

Now I must give some explanation of the motives that have induced me to deliver to the public the secrets of a heart belonging to a person whom I didn't know. It would be fine if I had been his friend: everyone understands the treacherous indiscretions of a true friend. But I had only seen him once in my life on the highway. Hence I cannot attempt that inexpressible hatred, which, hiding under the guise of friendship, awaits only the death or misfortune of its beloved object to unleash a torrent of reproach, counsel, mockery and pity on its head.

As I read these notes again, I am convinced by the sincerity of this man who so relentlessly displayed his personal weaknesses and defects for all to see. The story of a man's soul, even the pettiest of souls, is only slightly less intriguing and edifying than the history of an entire people, especially when it is a product of the observations of a ripe mind about itself, and when it is written without the vain desire to excite sympathy or astonishment. Rousseau's confessions[1] have their shortcomings in the fact that he read them to his friends.

So it was only the desire to be of use that made me print excerpts from these diaries, which I came by accidentally. Though I changed all the proper names, those about whom the diaries speak will likely recognize themselves, and perhaps they will find some justification for the behavior of which this man has long been accused—he, who henceforth will partake of nothing in this world of ours. We almost always forgive those we understand.

I have put in this book only that which is related to Pechorin's sojourn in the Caucasus. In my hands remains another fat book of diaries, where he tells his whole life's story. At some point, it too will receive the world's verdict. But presently, I do not dare to assume that responsibility for many important reasons.

Perhaps several readers will want to know my opinion of Pechorin's character? My reply is the title of this book. "What vicious irony!" they will say. I don't know.

I

TAMAN

Taman is the foulest little town of all the seaside towns of Russia. I almost died of hunger there, and even worse, the people there tried to drown me. I arrived late at night by stagecoach. The coach driver halted our tired *troika* at the gate of the only stone house at the town's entrance. The sentry, a Black Sea Cossack, having heard the sound of the horses' bells, issued his usual inquiry with a wild cry of "who goes there?" A sergeant and a corporal came out. I explained to them that I was an officer, and that I was traveling on official business to an active detachment and requested government quarters. The corporal took us through the town. Whenever we approached an *izba*[1] it was occupied. It was cold, I hadn't slept for three nights, I was exhausted and I started to get angry. "Take me somewhere you rascal! Even if it's to hell, just take me somewhere!" I cried. "There is one last *fatera,*"[2] responded the corporal, scratching the back of his head, "but your honor won't like it—it's unclean!" Having not understood the exact meaning of this last word, I ordered him to march on, and after long wandering through muddy alleys, where I could see only decrepit fences on either side, we drove up to a small peasant house, right on the sea.

A full moon shone on the reed roof and white walls of my new living quarters. Another peasant house, smaller and more ancient, stood next to it in a courtyard, which was enclosed by a stone wall. The land fell away in a precipice to the sea at the very walls of this peasant house, and dark-blue waves lapped below with relentless murmurings. The moon quietly watched the element, which was restless but submissive to her, and under her light, I could make out two ships, far off-shore, whose black rigging, resembling a cobweb, was in mo-tionless silhouette against the pale line of the horizon. "There are ships at the pier," I thought. "Tomorrow I'll set off for Gelendzhik."

A Cossack from the front line was fulfilling the duties of an orderly under my command. Having instructed him to un-load my valise and release the coach driver, I called the pro-prietor. Silence. I knocked. Silence. What was this? At last, a boy of about fourteen years crawled out of the vestibule.

"Where is the proprietor?"

"No." The boy spoke in a Ukrainian dialect.

"What? He's not here at all?"

"Not at all."

"And the proprietress?"

"Run off to the *slobodka*."[3]

"Who then will open the door for me?" I said, kicking it with my foot. The door opened. A dampness blew softly from the peasant house. I struck a sulfur match and put it up to the boy's nose. It illuminated two white eyes. He was blind, com-pletely blind from birth. He stood in front of me without moving, and I began to scrutinize the features of his face.

I confess that I have a strong prejudice against the blind, the cross-eyed, the deaf, the mute, the legless, the armless, the hunch-backed and the like. I have noticed that there is always a sort of strange relationship between the exterior of a person and his soul. It is as if, with the loss of a feature, the soul loses some kind of sensibility.

I started to scrutinize the face of this blind boy. But what would you suggest I read in a face that has no eyes? . . . I looked at him with involuntary pity for a while, when sud-denly a barely visible smile scampered across his thin lips, and, I don't know why, but it produced in me a most unpleasant impression. The suspicion that this blind boy wasn't as blind as he seemed was born in my mind. In vain I tried to persuade myself that you couldn't mimic a walleye, and why would you? But what was I to do? I am often prone to prejudice . . .

"Are you the son of the proprietress?" I asked him eventually.

"No."

"Who are you then?"

"An orphan, a cripple."

"And does the proprietress have children?"

"No. There was a daughter, ran away cross the sea with a Tatar."

"Which Tatar?"

"The devil knows! A Crimean Tatar, a boatman from Kerchi."

I went into the shack. The sum total of furniture inside consisted of two benches and a table and an enormous trunk by the stove. There wasn't a single image on the wall—a bad sign! The sea wind burst into the room through a broken windowpane. I pulled the end of a wax candle out of my valise and, having lit it, started to unpack my things, putting my saber and rifle down in the corner. I put my pistols on the table, spread out my felt cloak on the bench, while my Cossack put his on the other. After ten minutes he started snoring, but I couldn't get to sleep. In the darkness the boy with the wall-eyes continued to circle before me.

Thus an hour passed. The moon shone through the window, and its light played on the earthen floor of the peasant house. Suddenly, a shadow flew through a bright ray that cut across the floor. I half-rose and looked through the window. Someone ran past it a second time and hid God knows where. I couldn't imagine that this being had run down the steep slope to the water; however, there was nowhere else to go. I stood up, threw on my *beshmet,* girded myself with my dagger-belt, and quietly exited the peasant house. The blind boy was standing in front of me. I hid by the fence, and with a sure but careful gait he walked past me. He was carrying some kind of bundle under his arm, and turning toward the jetty, he descended a narrow and steep path. "On that day the dumb shall cry out and the blind shall see,"[4] I thought, following him at a distance from which I wouldn't lose sight of him.

In the meantime, the moon was becoming shrouded in clouds, and a fog rose on the sea. The lamp on the stern of the nearest ship just barely shined through it—and closer to shore, foam glittered on the boulders, which threatened to sink it at any moment. I descended with difficulty, stole down the steep slope, and this is what I saw: the blind boy paused, then turned right at the bottom. He walked so close to the water that it seemed as if a wave might grab him and take him away at any moment. But it was evident that this wasn't his first walk along these parts, judging from the conviction with which he stepped from stone to stone, avoiding the grooves between them. At last he stopped, as though he was listening for something, sat on the ground and put the bundle down beside him. Hiding behind a protruding part of the rock-face, I observed his movements. Several minutes later a white figure appeared on the other side of him. She walked up to the blind boy and sat next to him. The wind brought me their conversation from time to time:

"So, blind boy," said the female voice, "the storm is fierce. Yanko won't come."

"Yanko isn't afraid of storms," he replied.

"The fog is thickening," the female voice rejoined in a sad tone.

"Fog is better for getting past patrol ships," was the reply.

"And if he drowns?"

"Well then, on Sunday you'll have to go to church without a new ribbon."

A silence followed. But I was shocked by one thing: before, the blind boy had spoken to me in a Ukrainian dialect, and now he was expressing himself cleanly in Russian.

"You see, I'm right," said the blind boy again, clapping his palms, "Yanko isn't afraid of the sea or the wind or the fog or the shore patrol. Listen now. You won't fool me—that isn't water lapping, those are his long oars."

The woman jumped up and began peering into the distance with an anxious look.

"You're delirious, blind boy," she said, "I don't see anything."

I admit, as hard as I tried to make out in the distance anything that resembled a boat, I was unsuccessful. Thus passed about ten minutes. And then, a black dot appeared between the mountains of waves. It grew larger and smaller in turns. Slowly climbing up to the peak of a wave, and quickly falling from it, a boat was approaching the shore. Brave was the seaman who decided to set out across the strait at a distance of twenty *versts* on such a night, and important must his reason have been, to have induced him to it! Thinking this, with an involuntary beating of my heart, I looked at the poor boat, but like a duck, it dived under and then, rapidly waving its oars, like wings, sprang out of the depths in a spray of foam. And I thought to myself, it is going to strike against the shore with all its might and fly into pieces. But it turned deftly to one side, and hurdled unharmed into a small bay. A man of medium height, in a Tatar sheepswool hat, emerged from it. He waved an arm and the three of them took to dragging something out of the boat. The load was so great that even now I don't understand how it hadn't sunk. Each took a bundle onto his shoulder and they set off along the shoreline; and soon I lost sight of them. I had to go back, but I confess that all these odd things had perturbed me, and I barely managed to wait until morning.

My Cossack was very surprised to see me fully dressed when he awoke. I, however, did not give him any reason for it. I admired the blue sky beyond the window, studded with little clouds, above the far coast of the Crimea, which extended in a violet stripe and ended in a cliff, at the top of which a lighthouse tower shone white. Then I set off for the Fanagorya fort in order to learn from the commandant the time of my departure to Gelendzhik.

But alas! The commandant could not tell me anything definitively. The ships standing at the jetty were all patrol or merchant ships, which hadn't yet started loading. "Maybe in about three, four days, the postal boat will arrive," said the commandant, "and then we'll see." I returned home, morose and angry. I was met in the doorway by the frightened face of my Cossack.

"It's bad, Your Honor!" he said to me.

"Yes, brother, God knows when we'll get out of this place!"

He seemed even more alarmed at this and, leaning into me, said in a whisper:

"It is unclean here! Today I met a Black Sea *uryadnik*.[5] I know him—he was in my detachment last year. And when I told him where we were staying, he said: 'Brother, it's unclean there, the people are not good!' Yes, and it's true, who is this blind boy? He goes everywhere alone, to the bazaar, to get bread, to fetch water . . . it's clear that they're used to him around here."

"What of it? Has the proprietress appeared at least?"

"Today, when you were gone, an old woman came and with her a daughter."

"What daughter? She doesn't have a daughter."

"God knows who she was, if she wasn't the daughter. Over there, the old woman is sitting in her house."

I went into the peasant house. The stove had been lit and it was hot; a meal, a rather luxurious one for the likes of poor folk, was cooking inside it. The old woman answered all my questions with the reply that she was deaf and couldn't hear. What was I to do with her? I addressed myself to the blind boy who was sitting in front of the stove and putting brushwood in the fire.

"So, tell me, you blind imp," I said, taking him by the ear, "where did you trundle along to with your bundle last night?" Suddenly, my blind boy started to cry, scream, and moan.

"Where'd I go? Went nowhere . . . with a bundle? Which bundle?"

This time the old woman heard, and started to growl:

"Listen how they make things up—and about a cripple too! What do you want of him? What has he done to you?"

I was fed up with this and left, solidly resolved to find the key to this mystery.

I wrapped myself up in my felt cloak and sat by the fence on a rock, looking into the distance. The sea extended before me, still agitated from last night's storm. And its monotonous sound, similar to the murmur of a city falling asleep, reminded me of years past, and carried my thoughts northward to our cold capital city. Disturbed by these reminiscences, I sank into reverie . . . About an hour passed thus, or perhaps more . . . Suddenly, something that sounded like a song struck my ear. Yes, indeed, it was a song, in a fresh, little female voice—but where was it coming from? . . . I listen— the song is strange, sometimes drawn-out and sad, at other times quick and lively. I look around—there is no one anywhere. I listen again. It was as though the sounds were falling from the sky. I looked up: a girl with unruly braids wearing a striped dress was standing on the roof of the peasant house—a veritable *rusalka*.[6] Protecting her eyes from the sun's rays with her palm, she was peering intently into the distance, either laughing or saying something to herself or singing her song again.

I remember the song, every word of it:

> The ships pass,
> Their white sails,
> Over the green sea
> As though by charter free.
> My little boat
> With two oars,
> And no sails, slips
> Among those ships.
> If a storm strikes up
> The old ships
> Will raise their wing
> Over the sea spreading.
> I bow to the sea now
> Low very low,
> "Menace not this night,
> oh sea of spite:
> my little boat
> with its riches floats
> through the dark, blind
> with a wild little mind."

I was unwillingly subject to the thought that I had heard that same voice during the night. I was distracted for a minute, and when I looked up again at the roof, the girl wasn't there. Suddenly she ran past me, singing something different; and, snapping her fingers, she ran inside to the old woman and they began an argument. The old woman was getting angry and the girl guffawed. And then I saw my water sprite come running back again, skipping along. When she had come up beside me, she stopped and looked me intently in the eye, as if she was astonished by my presence. Then she went off to the jetty, casually and quietly. But that wasn't the end of the story. She circled my lodgings the whole day. And the singing and skipping didn't cease. Strange being! There were no signs of lunacy in her face. On the contrary, her eyes settled on me with a spry perspicacity, and those eyes, it seemed, were endowed with some sort of magnetic power; it was as if they were awaiting a question each time they looked at you. But as soon as I started to speak she ran off, smiling craftily.

I have definitely never seen a girl like her. She was far from being a beauty, but then I have prejudices with regard to beauty too. There was a look of breeding to her . . . breeding in women, as in horses, is of great matter. This discovery belongs to *La Jeune-France*.[7] It, beauty that is, not *La Jeune-France*, is in large part manifested in the gait, in the arms and the legs. The nose is especially telling. A straight nose is rarer in Russia than small feet. My songstress seemed no more than eighteen years old. Her figure had an unusual suppleness to it, she had a particular inclination of the head; she had long light-brown hair, a sort of golden tint to the slightly sun-tanned skin on her neck and her shoulders, and an especially straight nose. All this enchanted me. I read something wild and suspicious in her oblique gaze, and there was something indeterminate in her smile but such is the strength of prejudice: her straight nose had carried me from my senses. I imagined that I had found Goethe's Mignon,[8] the marvelous creation of his German imagination. Certainly there were many similarities: the same quick transitions between extreme agitation and complete motionlessness, the same mysterious utterances, the same leaping about, and strange songs . . .

Toward evening, I stopped her at the door and conducted the following conversation with her:

"Tell me, pretty girl," I asked, "what were you doing today on the roof?"

"Uh, I was looking to see whence comes the wind."

"What for?"

"Whence the wind, hence happiness also."

"What? Were you summoning happiness with your song?"

"Where there is song, there is happiness."

"And suppose you sing sorrow to yourself?"

"What of it? Where things aren't better, they are worse, and from worst to best is not far."

"Who was it that taught you this song?"

"No one taught it to me. As it occurs to me, so I sing. Whoever hears it, hears it. And he who should not hear it, won't understand it."

"And what is your name, my songbird?"

"Whoever christened me knows."

"Who christened you?"

"How should I know?"

"What secrecy! But I have found out something about you."

Her face didn't change, her lips didn't stir; it was as if the matter didn't concern her.

"I found out that you went to the shore last night."

And then, with great emphasis, I related to her everything that I had seen, thinking it would disturb her—not in the least! She burst into loud laughter.

"You have seen much, but know little. So keep it under lock and key."

"And what if I, for example, thought to take this to the commandant?" Then I adopted a very serious, even severe, stance. She suddenly leapt up, broke into song, and escaped like a little bird that has been flushed out of a bush. My last words were entirely inappropriate. At the time, I didn't suspect their importance, but afterward I had the opportunity to regret them.

As soon as it became dark, I ordered the Cossack to heat the kettle, as he would in the field, and I lit the candle and sat at the table, smoking from my traveling pipe. I had finished a second cup of tea, when suddenly the door creaked, and I heard steps and the light rustle of a dress behind me. I shuddered and turned—it was her, my water sprite! She sat down opposite me, quietly and wordlessly, and aimed her eyes at me, and I don't know why but this gaze seemed miraculously gentle to me. It reminded me of those gazes that, in the old days, had so tyrannically toyed with my life. She, it seemed, was waiting for a question, but, full of inexplicable confusion, I didn't say anything. A dull pallor had spread over her face, indicating a disturbance of the soul. Her hand wandered around the table without aim, and I noticed a light trembling. Her breast would rise up high at times; at other times she seemed to be holding her breath. This comedy had started to bore me, and I was ready to break the silence in the most prosaic way, that is, by offering her a glass of tea, when suddenly she jumped up, threw her arms around my neck, and a moist, fiery kiss sounded on my lips. My vision darkened, my head was spinning, I squeezed her in an embrace with all the strength of youthful passion, but she, like a snake, slipped from my arms, whispering in my ear: "Tonight, when everyone goes to sleep, go down to the shore." And like an arrow she ran out of the room, knocking over the candle and the kettle that stood on the floor by the entrance.

"What a she-devil!" cried out the Cossack, who was dreaming about heating up the remains of the tea, having made himself comfortable in the straw. Only then did I come to my senses.

After about two hours, when everything had fallen silent at the jetty, I roused my Cossack.

"If I fire my pistol," I said to him, "then run down to the shore."

He opened his eyes widely and replied mechanically, "Yes, sir." I thrust my pistol in my belt and left. She was waiting for me at the edge of the slope; her attire was very light, a small shawl wrapped around her lithe figure.

"Come with me!" she said, taking me by the hand, and we started to descend. I don't understand how I didn't break my neck. At the bottom we turned right and went down the very path along which I had followed the blind boy yesterday. The moon hadn't yet risen, and only two little stars, like two rescue beacons, glittered in the dark-blue vault of the sky. Heavy waves rolled in one after the next, rhythmically and evenly, barely lifting the little boat moored to the shore.

"Let's get into the boat," said my companion. I hesitated—I am not an enthusiast of sentimental outings on the sea—but it wasn't the moment to back down. She hopped into the boat, with me after her, and I hadn't quite come to my senses before I noticed we were drifting off.

"What does this mean?" I said angrily to her.

"It means," she replied, sitting me down on the bench and winding her arms around my shoulders, "it means that I love you . . ."

Her cheek pressed to mine, I felt her burning breath on my face. Suddenly something fell loudly into the water. I grabbed at my belt, but the pistol was gone. Oh, what a terrible suspicion crept into my soul, while blood surged to my head. I look around—we are about fifty *sazhens* from the shore, and I can't swim! I want to push her away from me, but like a cat, she had seized hold of my clothing and suddenly, with a strong shove, nearly threw me into the sea. The boat began to rock, but I got the better of it, and a desperate struggle began between us. Rage imparted me with strength, but I quickly noticed that I was inferior to my opponent in dexterity . . .

"What do you want?" I cried, firmly grabbing her little hands. Her fingers crunched, but she didn't cry out: her snakelike nature could endure such torture.

"You saw," she responded, "and you will inform!" And with supernatural exertion she toppled me to the side of the boat. We were both hanging over the edge of the boat from the waist. Her hair was touching the water. It was a decisive moment. I braced myself against the bottom of the boat with my knee and grabbed her braid with one hand and her throat with the other. She let go of my clothing, and I threw her into the waves in an instant.

It was already rather dark; her head flashed a couple of times in the sea foam; then, nothing more . . .

At the bottom of the boat I found half of an old oar, and somehow, after prolonged effort, got it moored to the jetty. Stealing along the shore toward my peasant house, I couldn't help glancing over to the place where yesterday the blind boy had waited for the night mariner. The moon had already rolled across the sky, and it looked to me as if someone in white was sitting at the shoreline. I crept up, with excited curiosity, and lay flat on the grass on top of the precipice, sticking my head a little over the edge. I could well see everything that was happening below from the cliff, and I wasn't much surprised, but was rather gladdened to recognize my *rusalka* there. She was squeezing sea foam from her long hair. Her wet slip outlined her lithe figure and raised breasts. Soon a boat appeared in the distance; it was approaching fast. A man wearing a Tatar hat stepped out of the boat as he had the day before, but his hair was cut like a Cossack's, and a large knife stuck out from the leather of his belt.

"Yanko," she said, "all is lost!"

Then their conversation continued but so quietly that I couldn't hear a thing.

"And where is the blind boy?" said Yanko finally, raising his voice.

"I sent him for something," was the answer.

The blind boy appeared after a few minutes, lugging a sack, which he put down in the boat.

"Listen, blind boy!" said Yanko. "You stay put here . . . you hear? Those are precious goods . . . Tell (I didn't catch the name) that I'm not his servant anymore. The matter went badly; he won't see any more of me. It's too dangerous now. I am off to find work in another place, and he'll never find a daredevil like me again. Yes, tell him that if he had paid better, then Yanko wouldn't have left. There are paths open everywhere to me, wherever the wind blows and the sea stirs!"

After a certain silence, Yanko continued. "She's coming with me. She can't stay here. And tell the old woman that it's time to die, she's lived longer than she should have, and it's time she went. And she won't see the likes of us again."

"And what about me?" said the blind boy in a plaintive voice.

"What are you to me?" was the reply.

In the meantime my water sprite had jumped into the boat and waved her hand at her companion, who put something in the blind boy's hand, saying: "Here, buy yourself some gingerbread."

"That's it?" said the blind boy.

"Here, have more."

The dropped coin rang out, striking against a rock. The blind boy didn't pick it up. Yanko sat down in the boat; a wind blew from the shore. They raised a small sail and tore off swiftly. For a long time the white sail flashed in the light of the moon amidst the dark waves. The blind boy continued to sit at the shore, and then something that resembled sobbing was audible to me: the blind boy was crying, and it went on for a long time . . . I became sad. Why had fate thrown me into this peaceful circle of *honest smugglers*? Like a stone thrown into a smooth spring, I had disturbed their tranquility, and, like a stone, I had barely avoided sinking to the bottom!

I returned to the peasant house. In the vestibule there was a burned-out candle on a wooden dish, and my Cossack, contrary to orders, was in a deep sleep, holding his rifle with both hands. I left him in peace, took the candle, and went into the peasant house. Alas! My case, my silver-worked saber, my Dagestani dagger (a present from a friend)—all had disappeared. Then I guessed just what things the damned blind boy had been lugging. Having awakened the Cossack with a sufficiently impolite shove, I scolded him, got angry, but there was nothing to be done! And wouldn't it be amusing to complain to the authorities that I had been robbed by a blind boy and nearly drowned by an eighteen-year-old girl? Thank God, there arose an opportunity in the morning to depart, and I abandoned Taman. What became of the old woman and the poor blind boy, I don't know. Yes, and what are the joys and calamities of man to me—to me, a traveling officer, equipped, even, with a road-pass indicating his official business!

(*The end of Pechorin's diaries*)

PART TWO

2

PRINCESS MARY

May 11

Yesterday I arrived in Pyatigorsk and hired quarters at the edge of town, at the highest point, at the foot of Mount Mashuk. When a storm arrives, the clouds will come right down to my roof. Today, at five o'clock in the morning, when I opened the window, my room filled with the scent of the flowers, which grow inside the modest palisade. The blooming branches of a cherry tree look at me through my window, and the wind strews my writing desk with white petals. The view in three directions is marvelous. To the west the five-headed Beshtau is shining blue, like "the last storm-cloud of a dissipating storm."[1] To the north rises Mashuk, like a shaggy Persian hat, covering one whole part of the horizon. Looking eastward is more cheering: below, a clean and new little town is flashing its colors, curative springs are babbling, the many-tongued crowd is babbling; in the distance an amphitheater of blue and cloudy hills towers over the town; and farther still, a silver chain of snowy peaks extends along the horizon's edge, beginning with Kazbek and ending with the two-headed Elbrus . . . What joy to live in such country! A kind of joyful feeling has spread to all my veins. The air is clean and fresh, like the kiss of a baby; the sun is bright, the sky blue—what more could one wish? What place do passions, desires, and regrets have here? . . . But it's time now. I am going to Elizabeth's Spring: it is said that the whole spa community gathers there in the morning.

————

I went down into the middle of the town and walked the boulevard, where I met several doleful groups going slowly up the hill. One could immediately guess by the worn, out-of-fashion frock coats of the husbands and by the refined apparel of the wives and daughters, that mostly these groups were the households of a landowner from the Steppe. It was obvious that the spa's young men had already been found and counted because they looked at me with a tender curiosity. My Petersburg-cut frock coat led them to an initial illusion, but as soon as they recognized the army epaulets they turned away with indignation.

The wives of the local authorities, the "mistresses of the waters," so to speak, were more gracious. They have lorgnettes, they pay less attention to uniform, and they are accustomed in the Caucasus to meeting ardent hearts beneath numbered buttons and educated minds under white military caps. These ladies are very charming and remain so for a long time! Every year their admirers are relieved by new ones, and this is perhaps the secret of their inexhaustible graciousness. Climbing the narrow path to the Elizabeth Spring, I overtook a crowd of men, civilian and military, which, as I later learned, comprised a particular class of people among those hoping to benefit from the action of the waters. They drink (but not the waters); they promenade little; they flirt but only in passing; they gamble; and they complain of boredom. They are dandies: they adopt academic poses as they lower their wickered glasses into the well of sulfurous water. The civilians among them wear light-blue neckcloths, and the military turn out the frills of their collars. They profess deep disdain toward provincial houses and long for the aristocratic drawing rooms of the capital where they wouldn't be admitted.

Finally, the well . . . In the little square next to it there is a small house with a red roof built over baths, and beyond that is a gallery where people promenade during rainstorms. A few injured officers sat on a bench, their crutches tucked up—pale, sad. A few ladies were walking to and fro with quick steps around the square, awaiting the effects of the water. There were two or three lovely little faces among them. Under the alley of vines obscuring the slope of Mount Mashuk, I could see the occasional flashings of a colorful hat, which must have belonged to persons who loved company in their solitude, since there was always a military cap, or one of those ugly round hats next to it. In a pavilion called the Aeolian Harp, which was built above a steep rock-face, the lovers of views hung about and directed a telescope at Mount Elbrus. Among them were two tutors with their pupils, come to be cured of scrofula.

I stopped, out of breath, on the edge of the hill and, leaning on the corner of a little house, I started to examine the picturesque environs, when suddenly I heard a familiar voice behind me:

"Pechorin! Have you been here long?"

I turn around: Grushnitsky! We embraced. I had met him on active service. He had been wounded by a bullet in the leg and had come to the waters a week before me.

Grushnitsky is a cadet. After just a year in service, he wears a heavy soldier's greatcoat—a particular kind of dandyism. He has the St. George's Cross for soldiers. He is well-built, has black hair and a dark complexion. He looks as though he is twenty-five years old, but he is barely twenty-one. He throws his head back when he talks and he twists his mustache with his left hand all the time, while the right hand leans on his crutch. His speech is quick and fanciful: he is one of those people who have a flamboyant phrase ready for any situation, who aren't touched by the simply beautiful, and who grandly drape themselves with extraordinary feelings, sublime passions and exceptional suffering. They delight in producing an effect. They are madly fancied by romantic provincial girls. Toward old age, they become either peaceful landowners, or drunks—and sometimes both. There are often many good attributes to their souls, but not a half-*kopeck* piece of poetry. Grushnitsky's passion was to declaim: he bespattered you with words as soon as the conversation left the arena of usual understanding; I could never argue with him. He doesn't answer objections, he doesn't listen to you. As soon as you stop, he begins a long tirade, which seemingly has some sort of connection to what you have just said, but which in fact is only a continuation of his own speech.

He is fairly sharp: his epigrams are often amusing, but they are never well-aimed or wicked. He will never slay a person with one word. He doesn't know people and their weak strings because he has been occupied with himself alone for his whole life. His goal is to be the hero of a novel. He has so often tried to convince people that he is not of this world but is doomed to some sort of secret torture, that he has almost convinced himself of it. This is why he so proudly wears his heavy soldier's greatcoat. I have seen through him, and for this he doesn't like me, even though on the exterior we have the most friendly of relationships. Grushnitsky has a reputation for being an excellent brave. I have seen him in action. He waves his saber, cries out, and throws himself forward, with screwed up eyes. This is something other than Russian courage!

I don't like him either: I feel that one day we shall bump into each other on a narrow road and it will end badly for one of us.

His arrival in the Caucasus was the consequence of just such romantic fanaticism. I am sure that on the eve of his departure from his father's village he was telling some pretty neighborhood girl with a gloomy look that he was going not just to serve in the army but that he was in search of death, because . . . and then he, probably, covered his eyes with his hands and continued: "No, you mustn't know this! Your pure soul will shudder! And why would I? What am I to you? Do you understand me?" and so on.

He himself has told me that what induced him to join the K—— regiment will remain an eternal secret between him and the heavens.

However, during those moments when he drops his tragic mantle, Grushnitsky is rather charming and amusing. I am curious to see him with women: here, I think, he will apply himself!

We greeted each other like old friends. I started to question him about the way of life at the spa and about its noteworthy personages.

"We lead a fairly prosaic life," he said, exhaling. "Those who drink water in the morning are sluggish, like all ill people, and those who drink wine in the evenings are intolerable, like all healthy people. There is female company but they don't provide much consolation: they play whist,[2] dress badly, and speak terrible French. This year, only Princess Ligovsky is here with her daughter, but I haven't met them yet. My soldier's greatcoat is like the stamp of an outcast. The sympathy it arouses is as oppressive as alms."

At that moment two ladies walked past us toward the well: one was older, the other young and well-proportioned. I didn't catch sight of their faces under their hats, but they were dressed according to the strict rules of the best taste: nothing extraneous. The second lady wore a high-necked dress in *gris de perles,* with a light silk *fichu*[3] twisted around her lithe neck. Little boots *du couleur puce* were tightened at her ankle, and her lean little foot was so sweet that even those uninitiated into the secrets of beauty would unfailingly have exclaimed "ah!"—even if only in surprise. Her light but noble gait contained something virginal about it that escaped definition, but it was decipherable to the gaze. When she walked past us, an indescribable aroma wafted from her, the kind that emanates sometimes from the letter of a beloved lady.

"That is Princess Ligovsky," said Grushnitsky, "and with her is her daughter, Mary, as she is called in the English manner. They have been here only three days."

"But you already know her name?"

"Yes, I heard it accidentally," he replied, blushing. "I admit that I don't want to be introduced. This proud nobility looks at us army-men like savages. And what is it to them whether there is a mind underneath this numbered military cap and a heart beneath this heavy greatcoat?"

"The poor greatcoat!" I said, bursting into laughter, "and who is the gentleman who is walking up to them and so courteously offering them a glass?"

"Oh! That is the Muscovite dandy Rayevich! He is a gambler: it is immediately obvious from the enormous gold chain, which coils around his light blue waistcoat. And what of the heavy walking stick—just like Robinson Crusoe! Yes, and his beard for that matter, and hair are *à la moujik*."[4]

"You are embittered against the whole human race."

"And for good reason . . ."

"Oh! Is that right?"

At that moment the ladies had walked away from the well and came up level with us. Grushnitsky managed to strike a dramatic pose with the help of his crutch and responded to me loudly in French:

"Mon cher, je haïs les hommes pour ne pas mépriser, car autrement la vie serait une farce trop dégoûtante."[5]

The pretty princess turned around and gifted the orator with a long and curious gaze. The expression of this gaze was very ambiguous but not mocking, for which I applauded her from my innermost soul.

"This Princess Mary is very pretty," I said to him. "She has such velvet eyes—yes, velvet. I advise you to appropriate this expression when speaking about her eyes. Her lower and upper eyelashes are so long that the rays of the sun don't reflect in her pupils. I love eyes that have no reflection; they are so soft, it's as though they stroke you . . . However, it seems that everything about her face is pretty . . . But now, are her teeth white? This is very important! A shame that she didn't smile at your magnificent sentence."

"You speak about pretty ladies as though they're English horses," said Grushnitsky with indignation.

"Mon cher," I replied to him, attempting to imitate his tone, *"je méprise les femmes pour ne pas les aimer, car autrement la vie serait un mélodrame trop ridicule."*[6]

I turned and walked in the other direction. For about half an hour I wandered along the grapevine alleys, along the limestone ledge, and among the shrubbery that hung between them. It was becoming hot, and I hurried back. Walking past the sulfurous spring, I stopped at the covered gallery to catch my breath in its shade, and this provided me with the occasion to witness a rather curious scene. The central characters were in this arrangement: the elder princess sat with the Muscovite dandy on a bench in the covered gallery, and both were engaged, it seemed, in a serious conversation. The young princess, probably having drunk her last glass, was strolling pensively by the well. Grushnitsky was standing at the well itself; and there was no one else in the little square.

I approached and hid in a corner of the gallery. At that moment Grushnitsky let his glass fall in the sand and then tried to bend down and pick it up—but his injured leg was in the way. Poor thing! How he was contriving, leaning on his crutch, making vain attempts. His expressive face really did convey suffering.

Princess Mary saw all of this better than I did.

Lighter than a little bird, she ran up to him, bent down, lifted the glass and gave it to him in a motion performed with indescribable charm. Then she blushed terribly, looked back at the gallery and, having reassured herself that her mama hadn't seen anything, calmed down immediately. By the time Grushnitsky had opened his mouth to thank her, she was already far gone. After a minute she came out of the gallery with her mother and the dandy, but assumed an air of utter propriety and importance as she passed Grushnitsky. She didn't even turn, didn't even notice the ardent look with which he long accompanied her, while she descended the hill and was eventually obscured by the linden trees of the boulevard . . . But then, her hat flashed on the other side of the street; she was running into one of the best houses of Pyatigorsk. The elder princess walked in after her and exchanged bows with Rayevich at the threshold.

Only then did the poor ardent cadet notice my presence.

"Did you see that?" he said, squeezing my hand tightly. "She is simply an angel!"

"Why?" I asked with an appearance of the purest sincerity.

"Didn't you see it?"

"No, I didn't see it. She picked up your glass. If the sentry had been here, he would have done the same, and even more swiftly in hopes of a tip. However, it's perfectly understandable that she was sorry for you. You were making such an awful grimace, when you stood on your wounded leg . . ."

"And you weren't at all moved, looking at her, at the moment when her soul shined through her face?"

"No."

I was lying, but I wanted to infuriate him. I have a congenital desire to contradict; my whole life is merely a chain of sad and unsuccessful contradictions to heart and mind. When faced with enthusiasm, I am seized by a midwinter freeze, and I suppose that frequent dealings with sluggish phlegmatics would have made a passionate dreamer of me. I will also confess that a feeling, unpleasant yet familiar, lightly ran over my heart at that moment—and this feeling was envy. I say "envy" boldly because I have become accustomed to admitting to everything; and you will rarely find a young man who, upon meeting a pretty girl who has captured his idle attention and discovering that she has suddenly singled out another man, equally unknown to her—you will rarely find, I tell you, a young man (it goes without saying that he lives in *le grande monde,* and is used to indulging his vanity) who would not be struck unpleasantly by this.

Grushnitsky and I descended the hill in silence and walked down the boulevard, past the windows of the house in which our beauty had hidden herself. She was sitting in the window. Grushnitsky, holding me by the arm, threw her one of those cloudy, tender looks, which have so little effect on women. I directed my lorgnette toward her and noticed that she smiled at his look, and that she was not at all amused but vexed by my impertinent lorgnette. How indeed could a Caucasian soldier have dared to point his piece of glass at a princess from Moscow . . .

May 13

Today, in the morning, the doctor came to see me. His name is Werner, though he is Russian. What is surprising about that? I knew a German who was called Ivanov.

Werner was an excellent person for many reasons. He was a skeptic and a materialist, like almost all medics, but furthermore he was a poet—I jest not. Always a poet in deed, and often in word, though he hasn't written two verses in his life. He has studied every living string of the human heart, like some who study the circulation of a corpse, but he has never been able to profit from his knowledge—like an excellent anatomist who isn't able to treat a fever! Usually, Werner ridicules his patients when they aren't looking; but I once saw him weep over a dying soldier . . . He was poor and dreamed of making millions but has not taken one extra step for money's sake. He once said to me that he would sooner do a favor for an enemy than for a friend, because for a friend it seemed like selling charity, whereas the generosity of an adversary only gives proportional strength to hatred. He has a wicked tongue, expressed through his epigrams; more than one good-natured person has gained the reputation of a vulgar fool as a result. His rivals, envious spa medics, sent out a rumor that he draws caricatures of his patients; the patients became enraged, and almost all of them refused to see him. His acquaintances, all truly decent folk who have served in the Caucasus, then strived in vain to resurrect his fallen credibility.

His appearance was one that strikes you, on first glance, as unpleasant but which subsequently becomes likable, when the eye has learned to read the stamp of an experienced and lofty soul in his irregular features. There have been examples of women falling madly in love with such people, who wouldn't exchange ugliness like his for the beauty of the most fresh and rosy Endymions. One must do justice to women: they have an instinct for a beautiful soul. That is perhaps why people like Werner love women so passionately.

Werner was short, thin, and as weak as a baby; one of his legs was shorter than the other, like Byron; his head seemed enormous in comparison to his trunk: he cropped his hair close, and the unevenness of his skull, exposed as it was, would have shocked a phrenologist with its strange weavings of opposing inclinations. His small black eyes, always agitated, sought to penetrate your thoughts. It was evident that there was taste and tidiness to his attire; his lean, veined hands stood out vividly in their light-yellow gloves. His frock coat, neck-tie and waistcoat were always black in color. Young men nicknamed him Mephistopheles. He acted as though he was angry at such a nickname but in actual fact, it gratified his vanity. We quickly understood each other and became friendly, because I am not capable of true friendship: one friend is always slave to the other, though often neither of them will admit it. I cannot be a slave, and to dominate in such a situation is an exhausting labor, because you must also lie at the same time. And besides I have a lackey and money! This is how we became friendly: I met Werner at S—— in a crowded and noisy circle of young men; the conversation toward the end of the evening took a philosophical and metaphysical direction; we were talking about convictions. Each one of us was convinced of this or that.

"As far as I'm concerned, I'm convinced of only one thing . . ." said the doctor.

"And what is that?" I asked, wanting to know the opinion of this person who had not yet spoken.

"Of the fact," he replied, "that sooner or later, one fine day, I will die."

"I am richer than you," I said, "as I have, apart from that, another conviction, which is that one very nasty evening I had the misfortune of being born."

Everyone found that we were talking nonsense, but, really, not one of them said anything any cleverer than that. From that minute, we had singled each other out in the crowd. The two of us often met and discussed abstract subjects that were very serious, neither of us noticing that we were but pulling the wool over each other's eyes. Then, having looked meaningfully into each other's eyes, as did the Roman augurs according to Cicero, we started guffawing and having laughed ourselves out, went our separate ways, satisfied with our evening.

I lay on the divan, aiming my eyes at the ceiling with my hand behind my head, when Werner came into my room. He sat in the armchair, put his walking stick in the corner, yawned and announced that it was becoming hot in the courtyard. I replied that the flies were bothering me, and we both fell silent.

"Note, dear doctor," I said, "that, without fools, the world would be very boring ... See, here we are, two intelligent people. We know in advance that we are each capable of debating to eternity, and so we don't debate. We know nearly all of each other's innermost thoughts. One word tells a whole story. We could see the kernel of each of our feelings through a three-layered shell. Sad things are funny to us. Funny things are sad to us. And in general, to tell the truth, we are indifferent to everything apart from our selves. And thus, there cannot be an exchange of feelings and thoughts between us. We know everything we wish to know about each other, and don't wish to know more. One solution remains: to discuss the news. Can you give me any news?"

Tired from my long speech, I closed my eyes and yawned ...

He thought for a while and replied:

"Well, there is an idea in that nonsense of yours."

"Two of them!" I replied.

"Tell me one of them and I'll tell you the other."

"Good, let's begin!" I said, continuing to examine the ceiling and smiling inwardly.

"You want details about one of the spa visitors, and I can guess which one you are bothering about, because there have been questions already about you, too."

"Doctor! We must absolutely not converse: we are reading each other's souls."

"And for the second . . . ?"

"The other idea is this: I wanted to make you recount something. Firstly, because listening is less tiring; and secondly, one mustn't be indiscreet; and thirdly, to learn the secrets of others; and fourthly, because intelligent people such as you like listeners more than they like storytellers. So then, to the matter at hand: what did old Princess Ligovsky say about me?"

"You are very sure that it was the older one . . . and not the young one?"

"Absolutely certain."

"Why?"

"Because the young one was asking about Grushnitsky."

"You have a great gift of understanding. The young princess said that she was certain that the young man in the soldier's greatcoat was reduced to the ranks on account of a duel . . ."

"I hope that you left her with that pleasant delusion."

"Of course!"

"We have a start!" I cried with rapture. "And we will take some trouble over the start of this comedy! Obviously, fate has taken upon itself to make things interesting for me!"

"I have a premonition," said the doctor, "that poor Grushnitsky will be your victim . . ."

"Continue, Doctor . . ."

"Princess Ligovsky said that your face is familiar. I remarked to her that she had probably met you in St. Petersburg, somewhere in social circles . . . I told her your name . . . It was familiar to her. It seems that your story has made quite a lot of noise there . . . The princess continued to describe your escapades, adding, in all likelihood, her own observations to society gossip . . . The daughter listened with interest. In her imagination, you grew into the hero of one of those new novels . . . I didn't contradict the princess, even though I knew that she was talking nonsense."

"My worthy friend!" I said, offering him my hand.

The doctor shook it with feeling, and continued:

"If you like, I'll introduce you . . ."

"Good gracious!" I said, raising my hands. "Do heroes really get introduced? Do they not become acquainted as they save their beloved from certain death . . . ?"

"And you really want to court the princess?"

"On the contrary, absolutely on the contrary! Doctor, finally I have triumphed: you don't understand me!" I continued after a minute of silence: "But this distresses me, Doctor . . . I have never exposed my secrets, but I do awfully like it when they are guessed because, in that case, I can always deny them when something happens. However, you must describe mother and daughter to me. How are they as people?"

"Firstly, the Princess Ligovsky is a lady of forty-five years," said Werner, "and she has excellent digestion, but her blood is contaminated. She has red dots on her cheeks. She has spent the last half of her life so far in Moscow and now, in retirement, she has grown fat. She loves naughty anecdotes and she herself sometimes speaks of indecent things when her daughter is not in the room. She conveyed to me that her daughter is as innocent as a dove. What was it to me? . . . I was moved to say something in reply—that I wouldn't tell anyone, to ensure her peace of mind! The Princess Ligovsky is being treated for rheumatism, and the daughter for goodness knows what. I ordered them both to drink two glasses of sulfurous water a day and to bathe in a diluted bath twice a week. The Princess Ligovsky, it seems, is not used to orders. She has a respect for the intelligence and knowledge of her daughter, who has read Byron in English and knows algebra. In Moscow, the young ladies have embarked on learning and it is a good thing, I'd say! Our men are so impolite in general, that to have to flirt with them must be unbearable to a clever woman. The Princess Ligovsky likes young men, but the young Princess Mary looks at them with a certain contempt: a Muscovite habit! In Moscow, they have only forty-year-old wits for their consumption."

"Have you been to Moscow, doctor?"

"Yes, I have practiced there a bit."

"Continue."

"Well, I have said everything, it seems . . . Yes! One more thing: the young princess, it seems, loves to discuss feelings, passions, and the like . . . She was in Petersburg for a winter, and it didn't please her, especially the society there. I suppose they received her coldly."

"You didn't see anyone with them today?"

"On the contrary: there was one adjutant, one tense-looking guardsman, and a lady who has just arrived, a relative of the princess by marriage, very pretty, but very poorly, it seems . . . Didn't you meet her at the well? She is of medium height, fair, with regular features and a consumptive color to her face, and there is a mole on her right cheek. Her expressive face is most striking."

"A mole!" I muttered through my teeth. "Really?"

The doctor looked at me and said solemnly, putting his hand on my heart: "You are acquainted with her . . . !"

Indeed, my heart was beating more strongly than usual.

"Now it is your turn to celebrate!" I said. "Only I am counting on you: don't lie to me. I haven't yet seen her, but I am sure that I recognize a certain woman in your portrait, whom I loved in days of old . . . But do not breathe a word about me to her; if she asks, treat me with disdain."

"As you like!" said Werner, shrugging his shoulders.

When he left, a terrible sadness squeezed my heart. Had fate led us again to the Caucasus, or had she purposefully come here, knowing she would find me? . . . And how will we meet? . . . And also, is it really her? . . . My sense of premonition has never lied to me. There isn't a person in the world over whom the past gains such power as it does over me. Every memory of a past sorrow or joy hits my soul painfully and elicits from it the same sounds it once did . . . I am a foolish creature: I don't forget anything—ever!

After dinner, at about six o'clock, I went to the boulevard: there was a crowd. Princess Ligovsky and Princess Mary sat on a bench, surrounded by young men, who were vying with one another to pay them their compliments. I placed myself on another bench at some distance and stopped two officers from the D—— regiment whom I knew, and started to tell them something. Obviously it was funny because they started to laugh as loudly as lunatics. The curiosity of several of those surrounding the young princess was piqued. One by one, they all abandoned her and joined my circle. I didn't stop: my anecdotes were so clever that they were silly; my mockeries of the eccentrics walking past were mean to the point of brutality . . . I continued to entertain the public until the sun went down. Several times, the young princess walked past with her mother, arm in arm, accompanied by some limping little old man. Several times her gaze, falling on me, expressed contempt while trying to express indifference . . .

"What stories was he telling?" she asked one of the young people who turned to her in politeness. "I suppose it was a very enthralling story—about his victory in battle . . . ?" she said rather loudly and, probably, with the intention of taunting me.

"Aha," I thought, "you have become angry indeed, dear princess; but wait, there is more!"

Grushnitsky followed her movements like a predatory beast—she didn't leave his sight. I'll wager that tomorrow he will be begging someone to introduce him to her. She will be very glad of it because she is bored.

May 16

Over the last two days, my affairs have progressed tremendously. The young princess decidedly hates me. Two or three epigrams at my expense have already been circulated, and they were rather biting but also very flattering. It is horribly strange to her that, accustomed as I am to good society, and as friendly as I am with her cousins and aunties, I am not making any attempt to become acquainted with her. We encounter each other every day at the well and on the boulevard. I make every effort, and do my utmost to distract her admirers—the shining adjutants, pale Muscovites and others—and I am almost always successful. I have always hated having guests but now I have a full house every day; they have dinner, supper, they gamble—and, alas, my champagne is triumphing over the power of her magnetic little eyes!

Yesterday, I encountered her in Chelakhov's shop. She was bargaining for a marvelous Persian rug. The young princess was entreating her mama not to begrudge her—this rug would decorate her dressing room so nicely! . . . I offered forty rubles more and bought it—and for that I was rewarded with a look that shined with the most ravishing fury. Near dinnertime, I ordered my Circassian horse to be led past her window, covered with this rug, just for fun. Werner was at their house at the time and told me that the effect of this scene was most dramatic. The young princess now wants to drum up a militia against me. I have already noticed that two adjutants bow to me very dryly in her presence, even though they dine at my house every day.

Grushnitsky has taken on a mysterious look: he walks around, with his hands behind his back, and doesn't acknowledge anyone. His leg has suddenly healed: he barely limps. He has found occasion both to enter into conversation with the Princess Ligovsky, and to give some sort of compliment to the young princess. She, evidently, is not very discriminating, because since then she has replied to his bows with the sweetest of smiles.

"You are resolute in not wanting to be introduced to the Ligovskys?" he said to me yesterday.

"Resolute."

"As you please! It is the most pleasant household at the spa! All the best society here . . ."

"My friend, I'm tired even of the best society that is not here. Have you been to their house?"

"Not yet. I have spoken twice with the young princess, not more, but you know, somehow it is not appropriate to impose oneself on a household, though it is done here . . . It would be another matter if I wore epaulets . . ."

"Come now! You are much more interesting as you are! You simply don't know how to make best use of your advantageous situation . . . That soldier's greatcoat makes you into a hero or a martyr in the eyes of any sentimental young lady."

Grushnitsky smiled in a self-satisfied way.

"What nonsense!" he said.

"I am sure," I continued, "that the young princess is already in love with you."

He blushed to his ears and puffed out his chest.

Oh vanity! You are the lever with which Archimedes wanted to raise the earthly globe!

"Everything is a joke to you!" he said, pretending to be angry. "Firstly, she knows me so little yet . . ."

"Women only love those that they don't know."

"Well, I don't have the least impression that she likes me. I simply want to make acquaintance with a pleasant household, and it would be very funny if I had any hopes . . . But you, for example, are another matter! You Petersburg conquerors: one look from you and the women melt . . . And do you know, Pechorin, that the young princess has been talking about you?"

"What? She has already spoken of me to you?"

"Well, don't start rejoicing yet. I somehow entered a conversation with her at the well, by accident. And her third comment was: 'Who is this gentleman who has such an unpleasant and oppressive gaze? He was with you when . . .'

"She blushed and didn't want to say which day, having remembered her charming gesture.

"'You don't have to tell me which day,' I responded to her. 'It will always be in my memory . . .'

"My friend Pechorin! I congratulate you: you are on her black list . . . and this is a shame indeed! Because Mary is very charming . . ."

It must be remarked that Grushnitsky is one of those people, who, in speaking about a woman with whom they are barely acquainted, will call her *my Mary, my Sophie,* if she has the good fortune to have taken their fancy.

I assumed a serious air and responded to him:

"Yes, she is not foolish . . . But be careful, Grushnitsky!

Young Russian ladies live on platonic love for the most part, without adding the thought of marriage to it. And platonic love is the most unsettling of all. The young princess, it seems, is one of those ladies who want you to entertain them. If they are bored with you for more than two minutes in a row, then you are irretrievably finished. Your silence must excite her curiosity, your conversation should never quench it. You must continue to disturb her with every passing minute. She will disregard considered opinion for you ten times in public, then call it a sacrifice; and in order to reward herself for it, she will torment you, and afterward will simply say that she cannot stand you. If you don't gain power over her, then her first kiss will not give you the right to a second. She will flirt with you abundantly, and after about two years she will marry a monster, out of deference to her mother, and will start to convince herself that she is wretched, that she only loved one person—you, that is—but that the heavens didn't unite her with him, because he wore a soldier's greatcoat, though under that thick, gray greatcoat, an ardent and noble heart was beating . . ."

Grushnitsky banged his fist on the table and started to pace the room.

I was laughing loudly inside and almost smiled twice, but he, fortunately, didn't notice this. It was clear that he was in love, because he became even more gullible than before. He even began to wear a silver ring with black enamel, made locally. It seemed a little dubious to me . . . I started to scrutinize it and what did I see? . . . Engraved on the inside in tiny letters, was the name "Mary," and next to it, the date of the day she picked up the famous glass. I hid my discovery. I don't want to force a confession from him. I want him to choose me as a confidante, and then I will really enjoy it . . .

Today I was up late; I arrived at the well—and no one was there anymore. The day began to get hot. White, shaggy rain clouds quickly sped down from the snowy mountains, promising a storm. The head of Mount Mashuk was smoking like an extinguished torch. Gray shreds of cloud twisted and crawled around it, like snakes, and they seemed to be held back in their strivings, as if they had been caught up in its prickly shrubbery. The air was filled with electricity. I went deep into the grapevine alley that led to a grotto; I was melancholy. I was thinking about the young woman whom the doctor had mentioned, with the mole on her cheek . . . Why is she here? Is it she? And why do I think that it is she? And why am I even convinced of it? Are women with moles on their cheeks so very rare? Thinking in this way, I walked right up to the grotto and looked: on a stone bench in the cool shadows of its entrance, a woman was sitting, wrapped in a black shawl, wearing a straw hat, with her head lowered onto her chest. The hat covered her face. I wanted to turn, in order not to ruin her daydreaming, when she caught sight of me.

"Vera!" I exclaimed involuntarily.

She shuddered and went pale.

"I knew you were here," she said.

I sat next to her and took her hand. A long forgotten feeling of awe ran along my veins at the sound of this sweet voice. She looked me in the eyes with her deep and peaceful eyes. They expressed mistrust and something like reproach.

"We haven't seen each other in a long while," I said.

"A long time, and we have both changed in many ways!"

"I assume you don't love me anymore?"

"I am married!" she said.

"Again? But this reason also existed a few years ago, and yet . . ."

She pulled her hand out of mine, and her cheeks blazed.

"Maybe you love your second husband?"

She didn't answer and turned away.

"Or he is very jealous?"

Silence.

"Well? He is young, handsome, special, faithful, rich, and you are afraid . . ."

I looked at her and became scared: her face expressed deep despair; tears were sparkling in her eyes.

"Tell me," she finally whispered, "is it fun for you to torture me? . . . I should really hate you. Ever since we have known each other, you have given me nothing but suffering . . ." Her voice trembled, she leaned toward me, and lowered her head onto my breast.

"Perhaps," I thought, "this is exactly why you loved me: joys are forgotten, but sadness, never . . ."

I hugged her tightly and we stayed like that for a long time. Finally, our lips approached each other and merged into a hot, intoxicating kiss. Her hands were as cold as ice, and her head was burning. Then one of those conversations started up between us, which don't make any sense on paper, which you can't repeat, and which you can't even remember. The meanings of the sounds replace and add to the meanings of the words, as in an Italian opera.

She absolutely doesn't want me to be introduced to her husband—the limping little old man whom I saw in passing on the boulevard. She married him for her son's sake. He is rich and suffers from rheumatism. I didn't allow myself to make even one mockery of him: she respects him, like a father—and will deceive him like a husband . . . It is a strange thing the human heart in general—and the female one in particular!

Vera's husband, Semyon Vasilievich G——v, is a distant relative of Princess Ligovsky. He lives near her. Vera is often a guest of the princess. I gave her my word that I would make acquaintance with the Ligovskys and would flirt with the princess in order to deflect attention from her. This way, my plans won't be spoiled in the slightest and it will be amusing for me . . .

Amusing! . . . Yes, I have already surpassed that period in a soul's life when it seeks only happiness, when the heart feels a necessity to love someone strongly and ardently. Now I only want to be loved, and at that, only by a very few. It seems to me, even, that one constant attachment would be enough for me—a sorry habit of the heart!

One thing has always been strange to me: I have never been a slave to any woman. On the contrary, I have always gained indomitable power over a woman's will and heart, absolutely without trying to do so. Why is this? Is it because I never prize anything and that they are permanently afraid to let me out of their grasp? Or is it the magnetic influence of a powerful organism? Or have I simply not succeeded in meeting a woman with an obstinate character?

I must admit that I absolutely do not like women of character: it is not their business!

It's true, I now remember: once, only once, I loved a woman with a firm will, whom I could never conquer . . . We parted as enemies—and yet, maybe, if we had met some five years later, we might have parted differently . . .

Vera is ill, very ill, though she doesn't admit to it. I am afraid that she has consumption, or that illness which they call *fièvre lente*—this is altogether not a Russian illness, and it has no name in our language.

The thunderstorm caught us in the grotto and kept us there for another half hour. She didn't make me swear my loyalty, didn't ask if I had loved any others since we parted . . . She put herself in my hands again with her former lack of concern—and I do not deceive her: she is the one woman in the world whom I would not have the strength to deceive. I know we will soon part again, and perhaps forever: we are following different paths to the grave. But the memory of her will remain inviolable in my soul. I have always repeated this to her, and she believes me, even though she says the opposite.

Finally, we separated. I followed her with my gaze for a long time, until her hat was hidden behind the shrubbery and the cliffs. My heart was tightening painfully, as it had after our first parting. Oh, how I was glad of this feeling! Could it be that youth wishes to return to me with its wholesome storms, or is this only its departing glance, its last gift, as a keepsake . . . ? It is amusing to think that I am still a boy to look at: my face, though pale, is still fresh; my limbs are well-built and lithe; my thick curls wave, my eyes glow, my blood stirs hotly . . .

Returning home, I mounted my horse and galloped into the Steppe. I love galloping through the long grass on a

hot-tempered horse, in the face of the winds of the desert. I
gulp the fragrant air with greediness and I direct my gaze
into the blue distances, trying to make out the cloudy details
of various objects, which become clearer and clearer with
every minute. Any bitterness that weighs on the heart, any
agitation that tortures the thoughts—it is all dispersed within
a minute. The soul becomes lighter, and the exhaustion of the
body conquers the anxiety of the mind. There isn't one female
gaze that I wouldn't forget upon looking at leafy mountains,
illuminated by the southern sun, or looking at the blue sky, or
noticing the sound of a waterfall, falling from crag to crag.

I think that the Cossacks, yawning in their watchtowers,
seeing me galloping without need or aim, would long be tortured by such a riddle, or, they would likely take me for a
Circassian, given my attire. I have actually been told that on
horseback, in Circassian costume, I look more Kabardin
than most Kabardins. And when it comes to this noble battle
attire, I am a perfect dandy: not one bit of extraneous galloon; an expensive weapon with simple finishings; the fur on
my hat isn't too long, too short; leggings and high boots fit-
ted to utter exactitude; a white *beshmet,* and a dark-brown
cherkeska.[7] I have long studied the mountain riding style:
nothing would flatter my vanity more than an acknowledg-
ment of my art in the Caucasian manner of horsemanship. I
keep four horses: one for myself, three for friends, to avoid
the boredom of roaming about the fields on one's own. They
take my horses with pleasure and never go out together with
me. It was already six hours after midday when I realized it
was time to dine. My horse was worn out. I went out onto the
road that leads from Pyatigorsk to the German colony where
the spa community often goes *en pique-nique.* The road goes
meandering between shrubs, descending into small gullies
where brooks flow under the canopy of the long grasses. The
blue masses of the peaks—Beshtau, Zmeinaya, Zheleznaya,
and Lisaya[8]—tower above and around like an amphitheater.
Having descended into one of the gullies, called *balkas* in the
local dialect, I stopped to let my horse drink. At that moment
a noisy and shiny cavalcade appeared on the road. There were

ladies in light-blue and black riding habits, and cavaliers in outfits made up of a mixture of Circassian and Nizhny Novgorod styles; and Grushnitsky rode at the front with Princess Mary.

Ladies of the spa still believe in the possibility of attacks by Circassians in broad daylight—that's probably why Grushnitsky hung a saber and a pair of pistols over his soldier's greatcoat. He was rather amusing-looking in these heroic vestments. A tall bush hid me from them, but through its leaves I could see everything and could guess from the expressions on their faces that their conversation was sentimental in nature. At last they approached the slope; Grushnitsky took the reins of the princess's horse, and then I heard the end of their conversation.

"And do you want to spend your whole life in the Caucasus?" the princess was saying.

"What is Russia to me!" replied her cavalier. "A country where thousands of people will look at me with contempt since they are richer than I am, when here, here, this thick greatcoat didn't prevent me from making acquaintance with you . . ."

"Quite the opposite . . ." said the princess, blushing.

Grushnitsky's face showed pleasure. He continued:

"Here my life flows past noisily, imperceptibly, and quickly, under the gunfire of savages, and if God would send me a bright female gaze every year, a gaze like the one . . ."

At that moment they came up beside me; I struck my horse with my whip and came out of the bush . . .

"*Mon dieu, un Circassien!*"[9] the princess cried out in horror.

In order to completely disabuse her of this, I replied in French, slightly bowing:

"*Ne craignez rien, madame—je ne suis pas plus dangereux que votre cavalier.*"[10]

She was embarrassed—but by what? By her mistake or by my reply, which may have seemed audacious to her? I would hope that the latter suggestion is correct. Grushnitsky threw me a look of displeasure.

Late that evening, at eleven o'clock that is, I went out for a stroll along the linden alley of the boulevard. The city was sleeping, the lights of fires flashed in a few windows. Craggy crests loomed black on three sides: the ridges of Mount Mashuk, on whose peaks lay a sinister little cloud. The moon smoked in the east. In the distance the snowy mountains sparkled with a silver fringe. The calls of the sentries alternated with noises from the hot springs, which are released at night. From time to time, the ringing clatter of horses scattered along the street, accompanied by the creaking of a Nogay wagon,[11] and doleful Tatar song. I sat on a bench and became lost in my thoughts . . . I felt the necessity to give vent to my thoughts in a conversation with a friend . . . but with whom?

"What is Vera doing right now?" I thought . . . I would give dearly to be holding her hand at this moment. Suddenly I hear quick and uneven steps . . . It's probably Grushnitsky . . . It is!

"Where have you come from?"

"From the Princess Ligovsky," he said very significantly. "How Mary sings!"

"Do you know what?" I said to him. "I'll wager that she doesn't know you're a cadet but thinks you were demoted . . ."

"Maybe! What is it to me?" he said absentmindedly.

"Well, I'm just saying . . ."

"And do you know that you made her terribly angry today? She felt it was an outrageous audacity. It took enormous effort but I managed to convince her that you are so well brought up and so well acquainted with society that you couldn't have had the intention of insulting her. She says that you have an insolent gaze, that you probably have a very high opinion of yourself."

"She isn't mistaken . . . and do you not wish to defend her honor?"

"I regret that I do not have this right yet . . ."

"O-ho!" I thought, "he obviously has hopes already . . ."

"But then again, it's worse for you," continued Grushnitsky. "Now it will be difficult for you to make their acquaintance—

a pity! Theirs is one of the most pleasant households I have ever known . . ."

I smiled inwardly.

"The most pleasant household to me is currently my own," I said, yawning, and stood up to leave.

"But you must admit that you are contrite?"

"What nonsense! If I so wished, I could be at the princess's house tomorrow evening . . ."

"We shall see . . ."

"And, in order to please you, I will even flirt with the princess . . ."

"Yes, if she deigns to speak to you . . ."

"I am waiting for the moment when your conversation bores her . . . Farewell!"

"And I am off to wander—I'm not at all able to fall asleep these days . . . Listen, why don't we go to the restaurant, where we can gamble . . . I need strong sensations today . . ."

"I hope you lose . . ."

I went home.

May 21

Almost a week had passed and I still hadn't made the acquaintance of the Ligovskys. I am waiting for a suitable occasion. Grushnitsky, like a shadow, follows the young princess everywhere. Their conversations are endless: when will she tire of him? . . . The mother isn't paying attention to this, because he isn't an eligible suitor. That is the logic of mothers! I noticed two, three affectionate glances—an end must be put to this.

Yesterday, Vera appeared at the well for the first time . . . Since we met in the grotto, she hasn't left her house. We lowered our glasses at the same time, and leaning in, she said to me in a whisper:

"Would you not like to meet the Ligovskys? . . . Only there can we see each other . . ."

A reproach! Boring! But I have earned it . . .

Incidentally: tomorrow there is a subscription ball in the hall of the restaurant and I am going to dance the *mazurka* with Princess Mary.

May 22

The hall of the restaurant had been turned into the Club of the Nobility. At nine o'clock everyone arrived. The princess and her daughter were among the last to appear; many ladies looked at her with envy and ill will because Princess Mary was dressed in such good taste. Those who consider themselves local aristocracy hid their envy and attached themselves to her. What is to be done? Where there is a collection of women, there will instantly appear a higher and a lower circle. Grushnitsky stood by the window, in a crowd of people, having pressed his eyes against the glass and now not allowing them to leave his goddess. Walking past, she nodded her head toward him just perceptibly. He beamed like the sun . . . The dances started with a *polonaise;* then they began to play a waltz. Spurs started ringing, coattails lifted and twirled.

I stood behind one fat lady, overshadowed by pink feathers; the splendor of her dress reminded me of the times of farthingales—and the mottled colors of her rough skin, of the happy era of black taffeta beauty spots. The biggest wart on her neck was covered by the clasp of her necklace. She was saying to her cavalier, a dragoon captain:

"This young Princess Ligovsky is a highly intolerable girl! Imagine, she bumped into me and didn't excuse herself, yes and she even turned and looked at me through her lorgnette . . . *C'est impayable!*[12] . . . And what does she have to be proud of? Someone needs to teach her . . ."

"No sooner said than done," the obliging captain replied and went off to the other room.

I then walked up to the princess, and invited her to waltz, employing the liberal local customs, which allow one to dance with unfamiliar ladies.

She could barely prevent herself from smiling and hiding her sense of triumph. She succeeded, however, quickly enough in striking a pose of complete indifference, even severity: she carelessly extended a hand to my shoulder, bending her head slightly to the side, and we were off. I haven't known a more voluptuous and supple waist! Her fresh breath touched my face; occasionally a ringlet, which had come loose from its friends in the whirlwind of the waltz, slipped across my hot cheek . . . I did three circuits. (She waltzes surprisingly well.) She was out of breath, her eyes had grown dim, and her half-opened lips could barely whisper the obligatory: "*Merci Monsieur.*"

After a few minutes of silence, I said to her, with a very humble air:

"I have heard, princess, that though completely unacquainted with you, I already have the unhappiness of having earned your disfavor . . . that you found me to be audacious . . . is it true?"

"And would you now like to confirm that opinion for me?" she replied with an ironic grimace, which, however, well suited her animated physiognomy.

"If I have had the audacity to offend you somehow, then let me have the even greater audacity to beg your forgiveness . . . And, really, I would very much like to prove to you that you are mistaken with regard to me . . ."

"That will be very difficult for you . . ."

"Why?"

"Because you don't visit us, and these balls, likely, will not be repeated very often."

This means, I thought, that their doors are forever closed to me.

"Do you know, princess," I said with a certain vexation, "one must never reject a penitent criminal: he might do something doubly criminal out of despair . . . and then . . ."

A guffaw and whispering in the people surrounding us forced me to turn and cut short my sentence. Several paces away from me stood a group of men, and in their number was the dragoon captain, who had just expressed hostile intentions toward the charming princess. He was especially pleased with something; he was rubbing hands, guffawing, and winking at his friends. Suddenly a gentleman in a frock coat with a long mustache and a flushed face separated from among them, and directed his unsure steps straight for the princess: he was drunk. Stopping in front of the embarrassed princess and putting his hand behind his back, he fixed his cloudy gray eyes on her and pronounced in a wheezy descant:

"Permetay . . . oh now what is it!? . . . Essentially, I'm reserving you for the *mazurka* . . ."

"What can I do for you?" uttered the princess in a trembling voice, throwing a pleading look around. Alas! Her mother was far away, and none of her friendly cavaliers were nearby; one adjutant, it seems, saw all this and hid behind the crowd, in order not to be caught up in the story.

"What?" said the drunken gentleman, winking at the dragoon captain, who was encouraging him with his gestures. "Aren't you game? . . . Then I again request the honor of engaging you for the *mazurka* . . . Maybe you think I'm drunk? No matter! . . . I can assure you it feels a lot more free that way . . ."

I saw that she was ready to faint out of fright and indignation.

I walked up to the drunk gentleman, grabbed him rather firmly by the arm, and, looking at him squarely in the eyes, requested him to move off. "Because," I added, "the princess long ago promised the *mazurka* to me."

"Well, what of it! . . . Another time!" he said, laughing, and withdrew toward his ashamed friends, who immediately led him off to the other room.

I was rewarded with a deep and miraculous look.

The princess walked up to her mother and told her everything, and the latter sought me in the crowd and thanked me. She declared to me that she knew my mother and was friendly with a half dozen of my aunts.

"I don't know how it has happened that we haven't met before now," she added, "but admit that you alone are to

blame: you avoid people as I have never seen a person do. I
hope that the air of my drawing room will chase away your
spleen . . . will it not?"

I gave her one of those lines which every one of us should
have prepared for such circumstances.

The *quadrille* went on for an awfully long time.

At last, the *mazurka* began to thunder from the balcony
above; the young princess and I seated ourselves.

I didn't once allude to the drunken gentleman, nor to my
previous behavior, nor to Grushnitsky.

The effect of the unpleasant scene slowly dissipated in her.
Her little face became radiant. She made sweet jokes. Her
conversation was keen, without the pretension of witticisms,
lively and free. Her remarks were sometimes profound . . .
I led her to feel, with a very intricate phrase, that I had long
ago taken a fancy to her. She bent her head and lightly
blushed.

"You are an odd person!" she said then, lifting her velvet
eyes to me and forcing a laugh.

"I didn't want to be introduced to you," I continued, "because there is too thick a crowd of admirers around you, and
I was afraid of disappearing in it."

"You needn't have been afraid! They are all very tedious . . ."

"All of them! Not all of them surely?"

She looked at me intently, as though trying to remember
something, and then blushed again lightly, and, finally, artic-
ulated decisively: "All of them!"

"Even my friend Grushnitsky?"

"Is he your friend?" she said, displaying a certain doubt.

"Yes."

"He, of course, isn't included in the ranks of the
boring . . ."

"But in the ranks of the unfortunate," I said, laughing.

"Naturally! Is it funny to you? I wish that you were in his
place . . ."

"What? I was once myself a cadet, and, really, that was
the best time of my life!"

"Is he a cadet?" she said quickly and then added: "But I thought he was . . ."

"What did you think?"

"Nothing! . . . Who is that lady?"

Here the conversation changed direction and did not return to this again.

Then the *mazurka* finished and we bid each other farewell with hopes to meet anew. The ladies dispersed . . . I went off to dine and encountered Werner.

"Aha!" he said. "There you are! I thought you wanted to become acquainted with the princess only while saving her from certain death?"

"I did better," I replied to him. "I saved her from fainting at the ball!"

"How is that? Tell me!"

"No, guess—o you who thinks he can guess everything in the world!"

May 23

At around seven o'clock in the evening I was strolling along the boulevard. Grushnitsky, seeing me from a distance, walked up to me: some kind of amusing delight was shining in his eyes. He shook my hand tightly and said in a tragic voice:

"I thank you, Pechorin . . . Do you understand me?"

"No. But in any case, you needn't thank me," I replied, not having any good deed on my conscience.

"What? And yesterday? Have you forgotten? . . . Mary told me everything . . ."

"What? Do you now share everything? Gratitude too?"

"Listen," said Grushnitsky very significantly, "please, don't mock my love if you want to remain my friend . . . You see: I love her to distraction . . . and I think, I hope, that she loves me similarly . . . I have a request of you: that you will be their guest this evening. And promise me that you will observe everything. I know that you are experienced in these things. You know women better than I do . . . Women! Women! Who can fathom them? Their smiles contradict their gaze, their words promise and beckon, but the tone of their voices pushes you aside . . . Within one minute they can understand and anticipate our most secret thoughts, and then miss the clearest hints . . . Take the princess: yesterday her eyes burned with passion, and they rested on me. Today they are cloudy and cold . . ."

"This might be the effect of the waters," I responded.

"You always think the worst . . . materialist!" he added disdainfully. "However, let us move on to other matters."

And, satisfied with his bad pun, he cheered up.

At nine o'clock we went to the Princess Ligovsky together.

I saw Vera at the window when I walked past her windows. We threw each other a fugitive look. Soon after us, she came into the Ligovsky drawing room. The Princess Ligovsky introduced her to me as her relative. We drank tea; there were many guests; the conversation was commonplace. I strove to ingratiate myself to Princess Ligovsky, telling jokes, making her laugh heartily a few times; the young princess also wanted to laugh more than once but held herself back, in order not to depart from her accepted role. She finds that languor suits her—and perhaps she is not wrong. Grushnitsky, it seems, was very pleased that my jollity did not communicate itself to her.

After tea, everyone went to the hall.

"Are you satisfied with my obedience, Vera?" I said, walking past her.

She threw me a look, full of love and gratitude. I am used to these looks—they once formed my bliss. The Princess Ligovsky sat the young princess at the piano; everyone asked her to sing something. I stayed quiet and made use of this commotion by going to the window with Vera, who wanted to tell me something very important concerning us both . . . It came out as nonsense . . .

Meanwhile, my indifference was vexing to the young princess, as far as I could tell from one angry, brilliant look . . . Oh, I understand this dialogue marvelously—mute but expressive, short but strong!

She sang: her voice was not bad, but she sings badly . . . though I wasn't listening. Grushnitsky, however, was leaning his elbows on the piano opposite her, and every minute saying under his breath, *"Charmant! Delicieux!"*

"Listen," Vera said to me, "I don't want you to become acquainted with my husband, but you must immediately ingratiate yourself with Princess Ligovsky. This will be easy for you: you can do anything you want to do. We will see each other only here . . ."

"Only?"

She blushed and continued: "You know that I am your slave: I was never able to resist you . . . and I will be punished for this: you will cease to love me! At least I want to guard my reputation . . . Not for my own sake: you know that perfectly well! . . . Oh, I beg you: don't torture me as you did before with empty doubts and feigned coldness. I may soon die, I feel that I am weakening from day to day . . . and despite this, I cannot think about a future life, I think only of you. You men don't understand the pleasure of a glance, a squeeze of a hand, and, I swear to you, listening to your voice, I feel such a profound, strange bliss, that the hottest kiss could not replace it."

Meanwhile, Princess Mary stopped singing. A murmur of praise distributed itself around her. I went up to her after everyone and said something to her about her voice that was rather offhand.

"I was even more flattered," she said, "to see that you didn't listen to me at all. But maybe you don't like music?"

"On the contrary . . . after dinner especially."

"Grushnitsky is right, when he says that you have the most prosaic tastes . . . and I see that you like music in a gastronomical respect . . ."

"You are again mistaken: I am not a gastronome at all. I have a particularly foul gut. But music after dinner lulls me to sleep, and sleep after dinner is especially healthy: there-fore, I like music in a medical respect. In the evening, on the other hand, it agitates my nerves too much: it makes me ei-ther too sad, or too merry. One and the other are so exhaust-ing, when there isn't a circumstantial reason to be sad or make merry, and besides, sadness in company is amusing, but an exaggerated merriness is not appropriate . . ."

She didn't continue listening until I had finished but walked right off and sat next to Grushnitsky, and some kind of sen-timental dialogue started between them. It looked as though the princess was responding to his wise phrases rather distract-edly and inappropriately, even though she was trying to look as if she were listening to him with attention, for he some-times looked at her with surprise, striving to guess the cause of the inner anxiety conveying itself occasionally in her uneasy glances . . .

But I have found you out, darling princess, beware! You want to pay me back in my own coin, and prick my vanity—but you won't succeed! And if you declare war with me, then I will be merciless.

Over the rest of the evening I interfered with their con-versation on purpose several times, but she would meet my remarks rather dryly, and with feigned vexation, I finally withdrew. The princess rejoiced in triumph; Grushnitsky did too.

Rejoice, my friends, and hurry . . . you won't have long to rejoice. What is to be done? I have a premonition . . . Upon becoming acquainted with a woman, I have always guessed, without error, whether she would love me or not . . .

I spent the remaining part of the evening next to Vera and we discussed every single thing about the past . . . Why she loves me so much, really, I don't know! Furthermore she is the one woman who has understood me completely, with all my small-minded weaknesses, my evil passions . . . Can it be that evil is so very attractive?

I left with Grushnitsky. On the street, he took me by the arm and after a long silence he said:

"Well?"

I wanted to tell him "you're a fool," but I held back and only shrugged my shoulders.

May 29

I haven't once diverted from my plan during all these days. The young princess has started to like my conversation; I have recounted several of my life's bizarre events to her, and she has started to see a rare person in me. I make fun of everything in the world, especially feelings: this has started to frighten her. She doesn't dare start up a sentimental debate with Grushnitsky in front of me and has already several times replied to his escapades with a mocking smile. But every time Grushnitsky comes up to her, I adopt a meek attitude and leave them alone. The first time she was glad of this or tried to seem so. The second time she became angry with me, and the third time—with Grushnitsky.

"You have very little self-regard!" she said to me yesterday. "Why do you think it is more fun for me to be with Grushnitsky?"

I responded that I am sacrificing my own pleasure to the happiness of a friend . . .

"And mine, too," she added.

I looked at her intently and assumed a serious air. Then I didn't say a word to her for the rest of the day . . . In the evening she was pensive; and this morning by the well she was even more pensive. When I went up to her she was absent-mindedly listening to Grushnitsky, who, it seems was delighting in nature, but as soon as she saw me, she started laughing loudly (very inappropriately), making it seem as if she had not noticed me. I went on a bit further and started to observe her stealthily: she turned from her interlocutor and yawned twice.

Grushnitsky has absolutely bored her.

I won't speak to her for another two days.

June 3

I often ask myself why I strive so doggedly for the love of young ladies whom I don't want to seduce and whom I will never marry! What is this feminine coquetry for? Vera loves me more than Princess Mary will ever love; if she had seemed an unconquerable beauty, then maybe I would be enticed by the difficulty of the enterprise . . . But not a bit! This is not that restless need for love, which torments us in the early years of youth and throws us from one woman to the other, until we find one that can't stand us. At that point our constancy begins—the true, everlasting love, which can be mathematically expressed with a line falling from a point into space—and the secret of this everlastingness lies in the impossibility of attaining its goal, that is, the end.

So why am I going to such pains? Out of envy for Grushnitsky? The poor thing, he doesn't deserve it at all. Or is this the result of that nasty but invincible feeling that makes us destroy the sweet delusions of a dear friend, in order to have the petty satisfaction of telling him, when in despair he asks you what he should believe: "My friend, I have had the same thing happen. And yet, as you can see, I enjoy dinner and supper and sleep very peacefully, and, I hope, I will be able to die without shouts and tears."

But there is an unbounded pleasure to be had in the possession of a young, newly blossoming soul! It is like a flower, from which the best aroma evaporates when meeting the first ray of the sun; you must pluck it at that minute, breathing it in until you're satisfied, and then throw it onto the road: perhaps someone will pick it up! I feel this insatiable greed, which swallows everything it meets on its way. I look at the suffering and joy of others only in their relation to me, as though it is food that supports the strength of my soul. I myself am not capable of going mad under the influence of passion. My ambition is stifled by circumstances, but it has manifested itself in another way, for ambition is nothing other than a thirst for power, and my best pleasure is to subject everyone around me to my will, to arouse feelings of love, devotion and fear of me—is this not the first sign and the greatest triumph of power? Being someone's reason for suffering while not being in any position to claim the right—isn't this the sweetest nourishment for our pride? And what is happiness? Sated pride. If I considered myself to be better, more powerful than everyone in the world, I would be happy. If everyone loved me, I would find endless sources of love within myself. Evil spawns evil. The first experience of torture gives an understanding of the pleasure in tormenting others. An evil idea cannot enter a person's head without his wanting to bring it into reality: ideas are organic creations, someone once said. Their birth gives them form immediately, and this form is an action. The person in whom most ideas are born is the person who acts most. Hence a genius, riveted to his office desk, must die or lose his mind, just as a man with a powerful build who has a sedentary life and modest behavior will die from an apoplectic fit. Passions are nothing other than the first developments of an idea: they are a characteristic of the heart's youth, and whoever thinks to worry about them his whole life long is a fool: many calm rivers begin with a noisy waterfall, but not one of them jumps and froths until the very sea. And this calm is often the sign of great, though hidden, strength. The fullness and depth of both feeling and thought will not tolerate violent upsurges. The soul, suffering and taking pleasure, takes strict account of everything and is always convinced that this is how things should be. It knows that without storms, the constant sultriness of the sun would wither it. It is infused with its own life—it fosters and punishes itself, like a child. And it is only in this higher state of self-knowledge that a person can estimate the value of divine justice.

As I re-read this page, I notice that I have substantially digressed from my subject . . . But what of it? . . . I am, after all, writing these diaries for myself, and therefore, whatever I throw into it, will become, in time, precious recollections.

———

Grushnitsky came in and threw his arms around my neck. He was made an officer. We drank champagne. Doctor Werner came in after him.

"I do not congratulate you," he said to Grushnitsky.

"And why not?"

"Because, the soldier's greatcoat suits you very much, and you have to admit that an infantry uniform, tailored here at the spa, will not bestow on you any allure . . . Do you see that until now you were an exception, and now you will join the general rule?"

"Goad me, Doctor! You won't stop me from celebrating. He doesn't know," added Grushnitsky in my ear, "how much hope these epaulets have given me . . . Oh, epaulets, epaulets! Your little stars, your little guiding stars. No—I am now completely happy!"

"Are you coming to walk with us to the chasm?" I asked him.

"Me? I will absolutely not show myself to the princess until my uniform is ready."

"Would you like us to make your joy known to her?"

"No, if you please, don't tell her . . . I want her to see me . . ."

"Tell me, then, how are matters between you and her?"

He became embarrassed and thoughtful: he had a desire to boast, to tell lies—and yet he was ashamed to lie. But he was also ashamed to admit to the truth.

"What do you think—does she love you?"

"Love me? For pity's sake, Pechorin, what notions you have! . . . How could that be, so soon? . . . Yes, and even if she does love me, then a proper lady wouldn't say it . . ."

"Good! And, in your opinion I suppose, a proper person should also keep silent about his passions?"

"Eh, brother! There is a manner of behaving in everything; a lot goes unsaid, but is guessed . . ."

"That is true . . . But the love that we read in the eyes does not oblige a woman as words can . . . Be careful, Grushnitsky, that she doesn't dupe you . . ."

"She?" he replied, lifting his eyes to the sky and smiling with self-satisfaction, "I feel sorry for you, Pechorin!"

He went off.

In the evening a large gathering set off to the chasm on foot.

In the opinion of the local scientists, this chasm is nothing other than an extinguished crater. It is located on the slopes of Mount Mashuk, one *verst* from the town. A narrow path leads to it between the shrubbery and crags; climbing up the hill, I gave my hand to Princess Mary, and she didn't let go of it for the whole remaining portion of the walk.

Our conversation began with gossip: I started to go through our acquaintances, both present and absent. At first I exposed their amusing sides, and then their bad sides. My bile was excited. I began by jesting—and finished with sincere malice. Initially this amused her, and then it frightened her.

"You are a dangerous person!" she said to me. "I would rather be caught in the forest under the knife of a murderer than by your tongue . . . I beg of you in all seriousness: when it occurs to you to speak badly about me, take a knife instead and stab me—I don't think you'll find it difficult."

"Do I really look like a murderer?"

"You are worse . . ."

I became pensive for a minute and then, adopting an air of being deeply troubled, said:

"Yes, such has been my lot since early childhood. Everyone would read on my face evil signs that weren't even there. But they were assumed to be there, and so they were born in me. I was modest—and I was accused of craftiness: I started to be secretive. I had deep feelings of good and evil. No one caressed me; everyone insulted me. I became rancorous. I was sullen—other children were merry and chatty. I felt myself to be superior to them—and I was made inferior. I grew envious. I was prepared to love the whole world—and no one understood me—and I learned to hate. My colorless youth elapsed in a struggle with myself and the world. Fearing mockery, I buried my most worthy feelings in the depths of my heart:

and they died there. I was telling the truth—and no one be-lieved me—so I started lying. Having become familiar with the world and the mechanics of society, I became skillful in the science of life, but I saw how others without such art were happy, blessed with the advantages for which I tirelessly strived. And then, despair was born in my breast—and not the kind of despair that can be cured by the bullet of a pistol, but a cold, impotent despair, masked by politeness and a good-natured smile. I became a moral cripple: one half of my soul didn't exist; it had dried out, evaporated, died. I had cut it off and thrown it away—while the other half stirred and lived at everyone's service, and no one noticed this because no one knew about the other half, which had died. But now you have awakened the memory of it and I have read you its epi-taph. To many, epitaphs are funny, but not to me, especially when I remember what lies beneath this one. However, I don't ask you to share my opinion: if my antics are funny to you—please laugh. I let you know in advance that it won't distress me in the least."

At that minute I met her eyes: there were tears running from them. Her hand, leaning on mine, was trembling. Her cheeks were glowing. She was sorry for me! Compassion—a feeling to which women submit themselves so easily—had sunk its talons into her inexperienced heart. She was distracted throughout the whole excursion and didn't flirt with anyone—and this was a great sign!

We arrived at the chasm; ladies abandoned their cavaliers, but she didn't let go of my hand. The witticisms of the local dandies didn't make her laugh. The steepness of the precipice at which she stood didn't scare her, while the other young ladies squeaked and closed their eyes.

On the way back I didn't resume our melancholy conversa-tion, and she responded shortly and distractedly to my empty questions and jokes.

"Have you ever loved?" I asked her toward the end.

She looked at me intently, shook her head—and again fell into reverie: it was obvious that she wanted to say something,

but she didn't know how to start. Her breast was excited . . .
What was there to be done? Her muslin sleeves were a weak
defense against the electric spark that ran from my arm to
hers. Almost all passions begin this way, and we often deceive
ourselves, thinking that a woman loves us for our physical
or moral attributes. Of course, these things prepare her heart
for receiving the holy fire, but it is still the first bite that de-
cides the whole matter.

"Wouldn't you agree that I was most cordial today?" the
princess said to me with a forced smile when we had returned
from the excursion.

We parted.

She was dissatisfied with herself: she had accused herself
of coldness . . . Oh, this is the first major triumph! Tomorrow she will want to recompense me. I know this all by heart
already—that's what's so boring!

June 4

Today I saw Vera. She bored me to tears with her jealousy.
The princess has taken it into her head, it seems, to trust
Vera with her heart's secrets: it must be said that that is a
happy choice!

"I can guess where all this is leading," Vera was saying to
me, "and it would be better if you just simply told me now
that you love her."

"And if I don't love her?"

"Well, then why are you pursuing her, alarming her,
agitating her imagination? . . . Oh, I know you well! Listen,
if you want me to trust you, then come to Kislovodsk in
a week's time. The day after tomorrow we will be going
there. The Princess Ligovsky will be staying here for the
meantime. Take an apartment nearby. We will stay in the
mezzanine of a big house near the source; downstairs will be
the Princess Ligovsky, and next door there is a house that
belongs to the same owner, which is not yet occupied . . .
Will you come?"

I promised, and the same day I sent someone to reserve the apartment.

Grushnitsky came to me at six o'clock in the evening and announced that tomorrow his full-dress uniform would be ready, just in time for the ball.

"At last I will dance with her the whole evening . . . then I will say everything that needs saying!"

"When is this ball?"

"Tomorrow! Don't you know? A big festival, and the local authorities have undertaken to organize it . . ."

"Let's go down to the boulevard . . ."

"Not on your life, in this ugly greatcoat . . ."

"What, have you ceased to love it?"

I went out alone and encountered Princess Mary, whereupon I invited her to dance the *mazurka*. She seemed to be surprised and glad.

"I thought that you only dance out of necessity, like the last time," she said, very sweetly smiling . . .

She, it seems, hadn't been noticing the absence of Grushnitsky.

"You will be pleasantly surprised tomorrow," I said to her.

"By what?"

"That is a secret . . . you will find out for yourself at the ball."

I finished the evening at Princess Ligovsky's house; there weren't any guests except Vera and one very amusing old man. I was in high spirits, and improvised various strange stories. The young princess sat opposite me and listened to my nonsense with such deep and strained yet gentle attention that I felt guilty. Where had her vitality gone? Her coquettishness, her caprice, her cheeky mien, her contemptuous smile, her absentminded look . . . ?

Vera noticed all of this: a deep sadness showed itself on her sickly face; she sat in the shadows by the window, sunken in a wide armchair . . . I started to feel sorry for her . . .

Then I recounted the whole dramatic story of our acquaintance, our love—but it goes without saying that I concealed all this with invented names.

I depicted my affection, my anxieties, my raptures so vividly. I painted her behavior and character in such an advantageous light, that against her will, she had to forgive me for my flirtations with the princess.

She stood up, came and sat with us, and livened up ... and it was not until two o'clock at night that we all remembered the doctor had ordered us to go to bed at eleven.

June 5

Half an hour before the ball began, Grushnitsky appeared at my place in the total brilliance of a full dress infantry uniform. There was a little bronze chain attached to his third button, on which hung a double lorgnette; his epaulets of incredible size were turned up like the little wings of Cupid; his boots squeaked; in his left hand he held brown kid-gloves and a military cap, and with his right hand he fluffed up the wavy tuft of his crested hair into little curls. His face expressed self-satisfaction with a touch of uncertainty. His festive appearance and his proud demeanor would have made me laugh if it had been in accordance with my plans.

He cast his military cap and gloves onto the table and started to pull down his coattails and to adjust himself in the mirror. He had an enormous black neckcloth, which was wound around an extremely high stiffener, the bristles of which supported his chin and stuck out half an inch above his collar. But it seemed to him that it showed too little so he pulled it up further, to his ears. Since the collar of his uniform was very tight, this great effort made his face fill with blood.

"They say that these days you are chasing after my princess awfully much," he said rather carelessly, without looking at me.

"What would fools like us be doing drinking tea?" I replied, repeating the favorite proverb of one of the cleverest rakes of a previous era, as once extolled by Pushkin.[13]

"Tell me, does this uniform sit well on me? Oh, that damnable Jew! How this cuts into me under the arms! Do you not have any perfume?"

"For pity's sake, do you need more? You already reek of rose pomade . . ."

"Never mind. Pass it here . . ."

He poured half the vial under his neckcloth, into his handkerchief and onto his sleeves.

"Are you going to dance?" he asked.

"I don't think so."

"I am afraid that I will have to start the *mazurka* with the princess—and I barely know even one of the figures . . ."

"Have you reserved her for the *mazurka*?"

"Not yet . . ."

"Careful that you have not been preempted . . ."

"Really?" he said, clapping his hand on his forehead. "See you later . . . I am going to wait for her at the entrance." He grabbed his military cap and ran off.

I set off half an hour later. The street was dark and empty; a crowd was squeezing around the hall or the tavern (whichever you'd like to call it); its windows were illuminated; the evening wind carried the sounds of a military band to me. I walked slowly. I was melancholy . . . Can it be that my single purpose on this earth is to destroy the hopes of others? Since I have been living and breathing, fate has somehow always led me into the dramatic climaxes of others' lives, as if without me no one would be able to die, or to come to despair! I have been the necessary character of the fifth act; I have played the sorry role of executioner or traitor involuntarily. What was fate's intent in all this? . . . Was I appointed the author of bourgeois tragedies and family novels—or collaborator to those who supply stories to the "Library for Reading"?[14] . . . How could I know? How many people begin life thinking that they will end it like Alexander the Great or Lord Byron, and yet remain a titular counselor for the duration . . .

Entering the hall, I hid in a crowd of men and started to make my observations. Grushnitsky stood by the princess and was saying something with great heat; she was listening to him absentmindedly, looking from side to side, putting her fan to her lips; her face expressed impatience; her eyes were searching for someone. I quietly walked up behind them, in order to listen to their conversation.

"You torture me, princess!" Grushnitsky was saying. "You have changed awfully since I last saw you . . ."

"You have also changed," she replied, throwing him a quick look, in which he couldn't discern the hidden mockery.

"Me? I have changed? . . . Oh never! You know that isn't possible! A person who sees you but once will forever carry your divine image away with him."

"Don't . . ."

"Why do you no longer want to hear what not long ago you frequently received so favorably?"

"Because I don't like repetition . . ." she said, laughing.

"Oh, I have been bitterly mistaken! . . . I thought, like a lunatic, that at least these epaulets would give me the right to hope . . . No, I would have been better off keeping that contemptible soldier's greatcoat forever, to which I perhaps owed your attention . . ."

"It's true, the greatcoat suited your face much better . . ."

At that moment I went up to the princess and bowed. She blushed slightly and quickly said, "Isn't it true, Monsieur Pechorin, that the gray greatcoat suited Monsieur Grushnitsky much better?"

"I don't agree with you," I replied. "Why, he looks even younger in his uniform."

Grushnitsky could not endure this blow; like all boys, he makes a pretense of being an old man. He thinks that there are deep traces of passion on his face that substitute for the imprint of years. He threw me a furious look, clicked his heels, and walked off.

"But admit," I said to the princess, "though he has always been amusing, not long ago you found him interesting too . . . in his gray greatcoat?"

She lowered her eyes and did not reply.

Grushnitsky pursued the princess the whole evening, dancing either with her or vis-à-vis. He devoured her with his eyes, sighed often, and exasperated her with his entreaties and reproaches.

By the third quadrille, she already detested him.

"I didn't expect this of you," he said, walking up to me and taking me by the arm.

"What?"

"You are dancing the *mazurka* with her?" he asked in a solemn voice. "She admitted it to me."

"And so? Was it a secret?"

"It stands to reason . . . I should have expected this from a girl . . . from a coquette . . . I will have revenge!"

"Blame your greatcoat or your epaulets, but why take against her? What is she guilty of—that she doesn't like you anymore?"

"Why would she give me hope, then?"

"Why did you have hope? To want and strive for something, I understand, but who entertains hopes?"

"You have lost the bet—only not completely," he said, smiling spitefully.

The *mazurka* began. Grushnitsky picked the princess only, and the other cavaliers picked her constantly too; there was obviously a conspiracy against me—all the better. She wants to speak to me, and is being prevented from it—then she will want it twice over.

I pressed her hand twice, and on the second time she snatched it away, not saying a word.

"I will sleep badly tonight," she said to me when the *mazurka* had finished.

"Grushnitsky is to blame."

"Oh no!" and her face became so pensive, so melancholy, that I swore to myself I would kiss her hand this evening without fail.

People started to leave. Having seated the princess in her carriage, I quickly pressed her little hand to my lips. It was dark, and no one could have seen it.

I went back into the hall, satisfied with myself.

Some youths were dining at the big table, and Grushnitsky was with them. When I came in, they all fell silent: they were obviously talking about me. Many had grumbled at me since the previous ball, especially the dragoon captain—but now they had definitely formed an adversarial gang against me, under the command of Grushnitsky. He had such a proud and brave look to him . . . I am very pleased. I love enemies, though not in the Christian way. They amuse me, excite my blood. Being always on one's guard, catching every glance, the significance of every word, guessing at intentions, frustrating their plots, pretending to be tricked, and suddenly, with a shove, upturning the whole enormous and arduously built edifice of their cunning and schemes—that's what I call life.

For the rest of supper, Grushnitsky conversed in whispers and winks with the dragoon captain.

June 6

This morning Vera left with her husband to Kislovodsk. I met their carriage as I was walking to Princess Ligovsky's house. She nodded at me: there was reproach in her look.

But who is to blame? Why wouldn't she give me a chance to see her alone? Love, like a fire, goes out without nourishment. Perhaps jealousy will do what my requests could not.

I sat at the Ligovskys' for a good hour. Mary didn't come out—she was unwell. She didn't appear on the boulevard that evening. Again, the newly-formed gang, armed with lorgnettes, assumed a really rather threatening look. I am glad that the princess was unwell: they would have done some impertinence to her. Grushnitsky had a disheveled coiffure and a reckless look to him. It seems he was genuinely distressed, his vanity was particularly offended—but it seems there are people in whom despair is even amusing!

Returning home, I noticed that something seemed to be missing. I hadn't seen her! She is unwell! Surely I haven't actually fallen in love? What nonsense!

June 7

At eleven o'clock in the morning—the hour when Princess Ligovsky is usually steaming in the Yermolovsky baths—I walked past her house. Princess Mary was sitting at the window, lost in thought. When she saw me she leapt up.

I went into the entrance hall; there was no one there, and I took advantage of the liberal local mores and forced my way into the drawing room without being announced.

A dull pallor spread over the princess's sweet face. She stood by the piano, with one hand on the spine of an armchair: this hand trembled slightly.

I quietly walked up to her and said:

"Are you angry with me?"

She raised a languid and deep gaze to me and shook her head. Her lips wanted to utter something and couldn't. Her eyes filled with tears. She sank into the armchair and covered her face with her hands.

"What is wrong with you?" I said, taking her hand.

"You don't respect me! Oh! Leave me in peace!"

I took a few steps. She straightened up in the chair, her eyes sparkling . . .

I stopped, having taken hold of the doorknob, and said:

"Forgive me, princess! I have behaved like a madman . . . it won't happen again. I will take measures . . . If only you knew what has been happening in my soul until now! You will never know, and all the better for you. Farewell."

As I left, it seemed to me that I heard her crying.

I wandered around the foothills of Mount Mashuk until evening. I became terribly tired, and, arriving at home, I threw myself on my bed in total exhaustion.

Werner came to visit me.

"Is it true," he asked me, "that you are marrying the Princess Mary?"

"What?"

"The whole town is saying it; all my patients are busy with this important news—these patients are quite a people—they know everything!"

"Grushnitsky is behind this trick!" I thought.

"In order to prove to you the falsity of these rumors, doctor, I will announce to you in confidence that tomorrow I am leaving for Kislovodsk . . ."

"And the Princess Ligovsky, too?"

"No, she is staying here yet another week."

"So you are not marrying?"

"Doctor, doctor! Look at me: surely I don't resemble a person who is betrothed or anything of the like?"

"I didn't say that . . . but you know, there are occasions . . ." he added, smiling cunningly, "in which a noble person is obliged to marry, and there are mamas who, at least, won't stand in the way of such occasions . . . And so, as your friend, I advise you to be more careful! Here, at the spa, the air is very dangerous. How many excellent young men have I seen, who deserve the best of success, and leave here to get married straight away . . . Even, believe me, some want to marry me! There was one mama in particular who was departing with her very pale daughter. I had the misfortune of telling her that the color would return to her daughter's face when she married. Then she, with tears of gratitude, offered me her daughter's hand and all her means too—fifty souls,[15] it seems. But I replied that I wasn't up to it . . ."

Werner left in the full certainty that he had cautioned me.

From his words, I noted that various nasty rumors regarding the princess and myself had spread in the town: Grushnitsky will receive his comeuppance!

June 10

It is already three days since I arrived in Kislovodsk. Every day I see Vera at the well and during the promenade. In the morning, upon waking, I sit in the garden that leads from our houses down to the well. The bracing mountain air has returned strength and color to her face. It is for good reason that the Narzan is called a mighty spring. The local residents confirm that the air of Kislovodsk disposes one toward love, and that all love affairs that begin somewhere in the foothills of Mount Mashuk have their denouements here. And it is true, everything here breathes seclusion; everything here is mysterious. The thick canopies of the linden avenues lean over a stream, which falls with foam and noise from rock to rock, cutting itself a path between the verdant mountains. The ravines, full of mist and silence, diverge like branches in all directions. The freshness of the aromatic air is burdened with the scents of the high southern grasses and the white acacia. And there is the constant sweet and soporific sound of the very cold streams, which meet at the bottom of the valley, chasing one another amicably, flinging themselves finally into the Podkumok River. On this side, the ravine is wider and turns into a green hollow, along which winds a dusty road. Every time I look at it, it seems to me that there is a carriage passing along it and that there is a rosy face looking out of its window. Lots of carriages do pass along this road, but that one hasn't appeared yet. The *slobodka* behind the fortress is densely settled; evening lights in the restaurant built on the hill a few paces from my quarters are starting to twinkle through two rows of poplars. Noise and the ringing of glasses stretch late into the night.

Nowhere do people drink so much Kakhetian wine and mineral waters as here.

> But there is a willing multitude
> Who mix these two occupations,
> I am not in their numbers[16]

Grushnitsky and his gang rage in the tavern every day and barely bow when they see me.

He arrived only yesterday but has already managed to argue with three old men, who tried to sit in the baths before him: misfortune definitely produces a warring spirit in him.

June 11

Finally they have arrived. I was sitting at the window when I heard the clatter of their carriage: my heart started . . . what was that? I couldn't be in love. Yet I am so inanely composed that you might expect something like this of me.

I dined at their house. The Princess Ligovsky looks at me very affectionately and doesn't leave the young princess's side . . . not good! But to make up for it, Vera is jealous of the princess's effect on me. To have attained such success! What a woman wouldn't do to upset a rival! I remember one girl that fell in love with me because I loved another. There isn't anything as paradoxical as a woman's mind; it's hard to convince a woman of anything, you have to lead them to convince themselves. The order of proof with which they destroy their caution is very original; to learn their dialect, you have to overturn all the rules of logic you learned at school. For example, this is the usual way:

This man loves me, but I am married: therefore I should not love him.

A woman's way:

I should not love him for I am married; but he loves me, therefore . . .

Here: an ellipsis, for common sense has already fallen silent. And most of the speaking is done like this: by the tongue, then the eyes, and, following them, the heart, if it is able.

What would happen if a woman's eyes were to fall on these diaries? "Slander!" she would scream with indignation.

Since poets started writing, and women have been reading them (and for this, profound gratitude is owed), women have been called angels so many times that, with heartfelt simplicity, they actually believe this compliment, forgetting that these are the very same poets who glorified Nero as a demigod for money . . .

It is inappropriate for me to speak about them with such malice—me, a man who has loved nothing in the world except them—who is always ready to sacrifice them for serenity, ambition, life . . . But it is not in a fit of annoyance and insulted vanity that I am trying to pull from them that magic veil, which only the practiced gaze can penetrate. No, everything that I say about them is only the result of

The cold observations of mind
And the sad remarks of the heart.[17]

Women should wish that all men knew them as well as I do, because I love them a hundred times more since I am not afraid of them and have comprehended their petty weaknesses.

Incidentally: the other day, Werner compared women with the enchanted forest, about which Tasso wrote in his "Liberation of Jerusalem."

"As soon as you set out," he said, "Heaven help you, such horrors fly at you from all sides: duty, pride, decorum, public opinion, mockery, contempt . . . You must not look, and you must just walk straight ahead and, little by little, the monsters will disappear, and a quiet and bright glade will open up before you, in the middle of which a green myrtle will blossom. But on the other hand, if your heart freezes at the first steps and you turn around then it is calamity!"

June 12

This evening was rich with incident. About three *versts* from Kislovodsk, there is a rock formation called the Ring, in a ravine through which the Podkumok River flows. It is a gate formed by nature; it rises up on a high hill, and through it the setting sun throws its last flaming glance to the world. A large cavalcade set off to see the sunset through this little rock-window. No one among us, to tell the truth, was thinking about the sun. I rode next to the princess; and on our way home, we had to ford the Podkumok. The smallest little mountain streams are especially dangerous because their depths are an absolute kaleidoscope: every day, they change due to the pressure of the waves; where a stone lay yesterday, today there is a hole. I took the princess's horse by the reins, and led her to the water, which wasn't more than knee-high; we gently started to advance along the diagonal, against the flow. It is well known that you mustn't look at the water when crossing a quickly flowing stream, for your head will immediately spin. I forgot to forewarn Princess Mary of this.

We were in the middle, in the rapids, when she suddenly swayed in the saddle. "I am not well!" she uttered in a weak voice . . . I quickly bent toward her, and threw my arm around her lithe waist. "Look upward!" I whispered to her. "It's nothing, don't be scared, I am with you."

She felt better. She wanted to be released from my arm, but I wound it even tighter around her delicate figure. My cheek almost touched her cheek. Flames wafted from her.

"What are you doing with me? Good God . . . !"

I wasn't paying attention to her quivering and embarrassment, and my lips touched her delicate little cheeks; she flinched but didn't say anything. We were riding at the back, no one saw. When we managed to get to the bank, everyone had already set off at a trot. The princess held her horse back. I stayed next to her. It was obvious that she was agitated by my silence, but I swore not to say a word—out of curiosity. I wanted to see how she would disentangle herself from this embarrassing situation.

"Either you despise me or love me very much!" she said finally with a voice containing tears. "Maybe you wanted to laugh at me, to perturb my soul, and then to leave. This would be so despicable, so base, that the supposition alone . . . oh no! Tell me," she added with a voice of tender confidence. "Is there something in me that denies me respect? Your audacious behavior . . . I should, I should forgive you for it because I allowed for it . . . Answer me, say something, I want to hear your voice!"

There was such female impatience in these last words that I smiled involuntarily. Thankfully, it had started to darken outside. I didn't answer.

"You stay silent?" she continued. "Maybe you want me to tell you that I love you first?"

I said nothing . . .

"Is that what you want?" she continued, quickly turning to me . . . There was something frightening in the resolve of her gaze and voice . . .

"What for?" I replied, shrugging my shoulders.

She struck her horse with the whip and went off at full speed along the narrow, dangerous road; it happened so quickly that I barely managed to catch up and then only once she had joined the rest of the group. She talked and laughed in alternation all the way home. There was something feverish in her movements. She didn't look at me once. Everyone noticed this unusual jollity. And the Princess Ligovsky was overjoyed inside, looking at her daughter. But her daughter was simply having a nervous fit: she would spend the night without sleeping and would weep too. This thought gave me immense pleasure: there are moments when I understand vampires[18] . . . But I also have a reputation for being a good fellow and aspire to this name too!

Dismounting from their horses, the ladies went in to Princess Ligovsky's house. I was agitated and I galloped to the mountains to disperse the thoughts that were thronging in my head. The dewy evening breathed a ravishing coolness. The moon was rising from behind the dark mountaintops. Every step made by my unshod horse resounded dully in the silence of the ravine. At the waterfall, I let my horse drink, and I greedily took two breaths of the fresh air of the southern night, and set off on my return journey. I passed through the *slobodka*. The lights in the windows were going out. The sentries on the ramparts of the fortress and the Cossacks on the surrounding picquets called to each other in long, drawn-out sounds.

I noticed an extraordinary light from one of the houses of the *slobodka,* which was built on the edge of the precipice; from time to time, the discordant sounds of talking and shouting rang out, indicating that it was a military carousal. I dismounted and stole up to the window; the shutters were not too tightly shut, which allowed me to see the revelers and to catch their words. They were talking about me.

The dragoon captain, flushed with wine, was banging his fist on the table, demanding attention.

"Gentlemen!" he said. "This is like nothing I've seen before. Pechorin needs to be taught a lesson! Those Petersburg fledglings are always giving themselves airs, until you hit them on the nose! He thinks that he is the only one who has lived in good society, since he always wears clean gloves and polished boots."

"And what of that haughty smile! I am convinced, meanwhile, that he is a coward, yes, a coward!"

"I think the same," said Grushnitsky, "and he likes a riposte. I once said a great deal of things that would have normally incited a person to hack me to pieces on the spot, but Pechorin addressed everything from an amusing perspective. I didn't challenge him, of course, because that was for him to do. Yes, and I didn't want to have any more business with him . . ."

"Grushnitsky is being vicious toward him because he snatched the princess away," someone said.

"What a thing to invent! It's true, I pursued the princess a little, yes, and I have now given it up, because I don't want to get married, and it isn't within my principles to compromise a young lady."

"Yes, I believe you, that he is a prime coward, that is Pechorin, and not Grushnitsky—oh, Grushnitsky is a clever fellow, and what's more he is my true friend!" said the dragoon captain again. "Gentlemen! Is anyone here going to defend him? No one? Excellent! And would you like to test his bravery? It will amuse us . . ."

"Yes, we would—but how?"

"Well, listen now: Grushnitsky is especially angry with him—so he has the principal role! He will find something wrong with some sort of silliness and will challenge Pechorin to a duel . . . Wait now, this is where it gets interesting . . . He will challenge him to a duel: good! And everything—the challenge, the preparations, the stipulations—will be as solemn and awful as possible. I will take care of this. I will be your second, my poor friend! Good! Only here is the hitch:

we won't put bullets in the pistols. I posit that Pechorin will lose his nerve—I will put them at six paces apart, damn it! Are you all in agreement, gentlemen?"

"Glorious plan! We agree! Why not?" resounded from all sides.

"And you, Grushnitsky?"

I awaited Grushnitsky's answer with agitation. A cold fury possessed me at the thought that were it not for this happenstance, then I would have been made a laughing stock by these idiots. If Grushnitsky hadn't agreed to it, I would have thrown myself upon him. But after a certain silence, he stood up from his place and, extending a hand to the captain, said very importantly, "Very well, I agree to it."

It is difficult to describe the rapture of the whole honored company at this.

I returned home, agitated by two different feelings. The first was sorrow. "Why do they all hate me so much?" I thought. Why? Have I insulted someone? No. Surely I am not one of those people who can incite ill will at first appearance? And I felt a poisonous malevolence, little by little, filling my soul.

"Watch yourself, Mr. Grushnitsky!" I was saying, walking up and down my room. "You can't play with me like this. You may pay dearly for the approval of your stupid comrades. I am not your toy!"

I didn't sleep all night. By morning, I was as yellow as a sour orange.

In the morning I met the young princess at the well.

"Are you unwell?" she said, looking at me intently.

"I didn't sleep last night."

"I didn't either . . . I have accused you . . . Perhaps it was unwarranted? But explain yourself, and I can forgive you everything . . ."

"Everything?"

"Everything . . . only tell me the truth . . . and quickly . . . Can't you see that I have thought about it so much, tried to explain everything, to justify your behavior. Maybe you are afraid of certain obstacles in the form of my relatives . . . This is nothing. When they find out . . . (her voice quivered) I will prevail upon them. Or is it your personal situation . . . but you know that I could sacrifice everything for the person I loved . . . Oh, say something quickly, take pity . . . You don't despise me—don't you?" She grabbed my hand. Princess Ligovsky walked in front of us with Vera's husband and didn't see anything. But we could be seen by the cure-seekers strolling past, the most curious scandalmongers of all, and I quickly freed my hand from her passionate grip.

"I will tell you the whole truth," I replied to the young princess, "I won't justify, nor will I explain my actions. I don't love you . . ."

Her lips paled slightly . . .

"Leave me alone," she said, only just distinguishably.

I shrugged my shoulders, turned, and walked off.

June 14

I sometimes despise myself . . . is that not why I despise others? I have become incapable of noble impulses. I am afraid to seem ridiculous to myself. Another person in my place would offer the princess *son coeur et sa fortune*.[19] But the word "marry" has some sort of magical power over me. As passionately as I can love a woman, if she gives me to feel even slightly that I should marry her—good-bye love! My heart turns to stone, and nothing will warm it up again. I am prepared for every sacrifice but this one. I would place my life on a card twenty times over—and my honor too . . . but my freedom I will not sell. Why do I value it so much? What does it do for me? Where am I planning to go? What am I expecting of the future? Exactly nothing, really. It is some kind of inborn fear, an inexplicable sense of foreboding . . . There are people who are instinctively afraid of spiders, cockroaches, mice . . . And shall I admit the truth? When I was still a child, an old woman told my fortune to my mother. She predicted that I would die at the hands of an evil woman. At the time, this struck me deeply. An insuperable disgust toward marriage was born in my soul . . . Meanwhile, something tells me that her prediction will come true. I will try, at least, to make sure that it comes true as late as possible.

June 15

Yesterday a conjurer called Applebaum arrived here. A long poster appeared on the doors of the restaurant, notifying the most venerable public of the fact that the above-mentioned conjurer, acrobat, chemist, and optician would have the honor of giving a magnificent performance on today's date at eight o' clock in the evening, in the noble assembly rooms (otherwise known as the restaurant). Tickets for two rubles and fifty *kopeck*s.

Everyone intends to watch the amazing conjurer. Even the Princess Ligovsky, despite her daughter's malaise, has taken a ticket for herself.

Today, after dinner, I walked past Vera's window. She was sitting on the balcony alone. A note fell at my feet:

> Today, after nine in the evening, come to me and take the grand staircase. My husband has left for Pyatigorsk, and he will not return until tomorrow morning. My men and housemaids will not be at home. I have given them all tickets, and the Princess's staff has gone too. I will expect you, come without fail.

"Aha!" I thought. "Finally things are turning out my way."

At eight o'clock I went to see the conjurer. The audience had gathered just before nine. The performance began. In the seats of the back row I recognized the lackeys and housemaids employed by Vera and the Princess Ligovsky. They were all here, every single one. Grushnitsky was sitting in the first row with a lorgnette. The conjurer addressed him every time he needed a handkerchief, a pocket-watch, a ring, and the rest.

Grushnitsky hasn't bowed to me for a while now, and the last two times he has looked at me rather impertinently. He will be reminded of this when it comes to settling our score.

Before ten, I stood up and left.

It was as dark as pitch in the courtyard. Heavy, cold clouds had settled on the pinnacles of the surrounding mountains. Only now and then, the dying wind sounded in the tops of the poplars, surrounding the restaurant. People were crowded around its windows. I went down the hill and hastened my steps as I turned into the gate. Suddenly it seemed that someone was following me. I stopped and looked around. In the darkness I couldn't make out anything. However, out of carefulness, I walked around the house, as though I was having a stroll. Walking past the Princess Mary's window, I heard steps behind me again. A person, wrapped up in a greatcoat, ran past me. This alarmed me. However, I stole onto the veranda and hurriedly ran up the dark staircase. The door opened. A small hand grasped my hand . . .

"No one saw you?" said Vera in a whisper, pressing herself to me.

"No one!"

"Now do you believe that I love you? Oh, I hesitated for a long time, I was tormented . . . but you can do with me what you like."

Her heart pounded; her hands were as cold as ice. The reproaches, the jealousies, the complaints began. She was demanding of me that I confess everything to her, saying that she would endure my betrayal with submissiveness, because all she wanted was my happiness. I didn't completely believe this, but I reassured her with my vows, promises, and so on.

"So, you are not marrying Mary? You don't love her? But she thinks . . . You know, she is madly in love with you, the poor thing!"

Around two o'clock after midnight I opened the window, and tying together two shawls and holding onto the column, I descended from the top balcony to the lower one. Princess Mary's lights were still lit. The curtain wasn't totally drawn, and I was able to cast a curious peek into the interior of the room. Mary was sitting on her bed, her hands crossed in her lap. Her thick hair was gathered up under a night bonnet stitched with lace. A big crimson kerchief covered her little white shoulders. Her little feet were hidden in colorful Persian slippers. She was sitting motionless, her head lowered onto her breast. There was an open book in front of her on the table, but her eyes were motionless, full of indescribable sadness, and it seemed that they had been running over one and the same page for the hundredth time, since her thoughts were far away . . .

At that moment, someone moved behind a bush. I leapt from the balcony onto the turf. An invisible hand grabbed me by the shoulder.

"Aha!" said a rough voice. "You've been caught! Visiting princesses at night, indeed!"

"Hold him tighter!" said another voice, jumping out from behind a corner.

This was Grushnitsky and the dragoon captain.

I hit the latter on the head with my fist, knocked him from his feet, and fled into the bushes. I was familiar with all the paths of the garden that covered the slope opposite our houses.

"Thieves! Help!" they cried. A rifle shot rang out. A smoking wad fell almost at my feet.

A minute later I was already in my room, undressed and lying down. My lackey had barely closed the door and locked it when Grushnitsky and the captain started knocking.

"Pechorin! Are you sleeping? Are you there?" yelled the captain.

"Get up—there are thieves about . . . Circassians!"

"I have a cold," I replied, "and I am afraid to make it worse."

They left. It was a mistake to respond to them: they would have looked for me in the garden for another hour. In the meantime a terrible alarm was raised. A Cossack came galloping from the fortress. Everyone stirred. They started to search for Circassians in every bush—and, it goes without saying, they didn't find anything. But I imagine many remained firm in the conviction that had the garrison demonstrated

more courage and haste, then at least two dozen of the pred-
ators would have been stopped in their tracks.

June 16

This morning at the well there was talk and nothing else about
the nocturnal attack of the Circassians. Having drunk the
prescribed number of glasses of Narzan, I walked the length
of the linden avenue about ten times and encountered Vera's
husband, who had just arrived from Pyatigorsk. He took me
by the arm, and we went to the restaurant to have breakfast.
He was terribly worried about his wife.

"How frightened she was last night!" he was saying. "And
that it would happen at the moment of my absence."

We settled down to breakfast by the door that led to a
corner room in which ten or so young men were sitting, and
amongst their number was Grushnitsky. Fate, for a second
time, had provided me with the occasion of overhearing a
conversation that was supposed to decide his fate. He didn't
see me, and therefore I couldn't be suspicious of his designs.
But this only augments his guilt in my eyes.

"It can't really be that they were Circassians," someone
said. "Did anyone see them?"

"I will tell you the whole story," replied Grushnitsky,
"only, please, don't give me away. Here is how it was: yesterday a man whom I won't name comes to me and tells me
that just before ten o'clock in the evening he saw someone
stealing up to the Ligovsky house. I must remark that the
Princess Ligovsky was here, but the young princess was at
home. So he and I set off to lie in wait for the lucky man under the window."

I admit that I took fright at this, even though my interlocutor was very busy with his breakfast: he could have
overheard things that would be rather unpleasant for him, if
Grushnitsky had guessed the truth. But blind with jealousy,
he didn't suspect it.

"So you see," continued Grushnitsky, "we set off just simply to scare him, having taken a gun with us, loaded with blank cartridges. Toward two o'clock we were waiting in the garden. Finally, and God knows where he appeared from, only it wasn't from the window, because it wasn't open—he must have come out of the glass door that is behind the columns—finally, I say, we see someone coming down from the balcony . . . What kind of princess can she be? Ah? Well, I do declare, young Muscovite ladies! After this, what can you trust? We wanted to capture him, but he broke free, and, like a hare, fled into the bushes. Then I shot at him."

A grumble of disbelief could be heard around Grushnitsky.

"You don't believe me?" he continued. "I give you my honest, noble word, that all this is the absolute truth, and in evidence, if you like, I will give the gentleman's name."

"Tell us, tell us—who is it, then?" could be heard from every side.

"Pechorin," replied Grushnitsky.

At that moment, he raised his eyes—I was standing in the doorway opposite him. He blushed horribly. I walked up to him and said slowly and distinctly:

"I am very sorry to have come in after you have already given your honest word in the confirmation of this disgusting slander. My presence saves you from further depravity."

Grushnitsky leapt up from his place and made motions of becoming impassioned.

"I request of you," I continued in the same tone, "I request of you that you retract your words right now. You know very well that this is a fabrication. I don't think that the indifference of a woman toward your shining merits deserves such terrible vengeance. Consider this well: in maintaining your opinion, you are losing the right to be called a noble man and are risking your life."

Grushnitsky stood in front of me, having lowered his eyes, in fierce agitation. But the struggle between his conscience and his vanity was short-lived. The dragoon captain, sitting next to him, nudged him with his elbow. He flinched and quickly answered me without lifting his eyes:

"Gracious sir, when I say something, then it is what I think, and I am prepared to repeat it . . . I am not afraid of your threats and am prepared for anything . . ."

"You have already demonstrated the latter," I replied to him coldly, and, taking the dragoon captain by the arm, I left the room.

"What can I do for you?" asked the captain.

"You are Grushnitsky's friend, and will be his second, I assume?"

The captain bowed very importantly.

"You have guessed it," he answered. "I am even obliged to be his second, since the insult caused to him concerns me too. I was with him yesterday night," he added, straightening his slightly round-shouldered figure.

"Oh! So it was you whom I hit so clumsily on the head?"

He turned yellow, then blue. The concealed spite showed on his face.

"I will have the honor of sending my second to you today," I added, bowing very politely and giving the impression that I wasn't paying attention to his fury.

I met Vera's husband on the terrace of the restaurant. It seems that he had been waiting for me.

He grasped my hand with a feeling that looked like delight.

"Noble young man!" said he, with tears in his eyes. "I heard everything. What a swine! Ingrate! . . . What proper household would entertain them after this?! Thank God I don't have daughters. But you will be rewarded by the young lady for whom you are risking your life. You can be sure of my modesty for the time being," he continued. "I was once young myself and served in the military—I know not to intervene in these matters. Farewell."

Poor man! He is happy that he doesn't have daughters . . .

I went straight to Werner, found him at home, and told him everything—my relations with Vera and with the princess and the conversation that I overheard, from which I learned the intention of these gentlemen to make a fool of

me, to make me fire blank cartridges. But now the matter
had departed from the boundaries of a joke. They probably
didn't expect such a result. The doctor agreed to be my second. I gave him several instructions concerning the stipulations of the duel. He should insist that the matter is worked
out as secretly as possible, because though I am ready to expose myself to death at any time, I am not in the least in-
clined toward ruining my future in this world forever.

After this I went home. The doctor returned from his mis-
sion an hour later.

"There is definitely a plot against you," he said. "I found
the dragoon captain and another gentleman, whose last name
I don't remember, at Grushnitsky's place. I paused for a minute in the entrance hall in order to remove my galoshes. There
was a terrible noise and argument going on inside . . .

" 'I won't agree to that for anything!' Grushnitsky was
saying. 'He insulted me publicly—before that it was entirely
different . . .'

" 'What is it to you?' answered the dragoon captain. 'I'll
take it all onto myself. I have been a second in five duels and
I know well how to arrange it all. I have devised everything.
If you please, just don't get in my way. Giving someone a
scare is no bad thing. And why expose yourself to danger, if
you can escape it?'

"At that minute I walked up. They went silent. Our negotiations lasted rather a long time; finally we decided the matter thus: about five *verst*s from here, there is a hidden gully.
They will go there tomorrow at four o'clock in the morning,
and we will depart half an hour after them. Shots will be at
six paces—this was requested by Grushnitsky. The dead body
will be attributed to the Circassians. Now, these are my suspicions: they, the seconds that is, have somewhat changed
their prior plans it seems, and they want to load a bullet into
Grushnitsky's pistol alone. This is a little similar to murder,
but in wartime, and especially an Asiatic war, such strata-
gems are allowed. Only Grushnitsky, it would seem, is a little
more noble than his friends. What do you think? Shall we
reveal to him that we have figured it out?"

"Not for anything in this world, Doctor! Be calm, I will not give in to them."

"What then do you want to do?"

"That is my secret."

"Watch you don't get caught . . . especially at six paces!"

"Doctor, I will wait for you tomorrow at four o'clock. The horses will be ready . . . Good-bye."

I sat at home until evening, and shut myself in my room. A lackey came to call me to the Princess Ligovsky—I ordered him to tell them I was ill.

Two o'clock at night . . . I cannot sleep . . . But I must fall asleep, so that tomorrow my hand won't shake. However, at six paces, it is hard to miss. Ah! Mr. Grushnitsky! You won't succeed in your hoax . . . We will swap roles. Now it is I who shall look for the symptoms of secret fear on your pale face. Why did you set yourself these fateful six paces? You think that I will offer you my forehead without a struggle . . . but we are casting lots! . . . But then . . . then . . . what if his luck outweighs mine . . . if my star has at last betrayed me? . . . It would be no surprise: it has faithfully served my whims for so long, there is no more constancy in the heavens than on earth.

So? If I die, then I die! The loss to the world won't be great. Yes, and I'm fairly bored with myself already. I am like a man who is yawning at a ball, whose reason for not going home to bed is only that his carriage hasn't arrived yet. But the carriage is ready . . . farewell!

I run through the memory of my past in its entirety and can't help asking myself: Why have I lived? For what purpose was I born? . . . There probably was one once, and I probably did have a lofty calling, because I feel a boundless strength in my soul . . . But I didn't divine this calling. I was carried away with the baits of passion, empty and unrewarding. I came out of their crucible as hard and cold as iron, but I had lost forever the ardor for noble aspirations, the best flower of life. Since then, how many times have I played the role of the ax in the hands of fate! Like an instrument of execution,

I fell on the head of doomed martyrs, often without malice, always without regret . . . My love never brought anyone happiness, because I never sacrificed anything for those I loved: I loved for myself, for my personal pleasure. I was simply satisfying a strange need of the heart, with greediness, swallowing their feelings, their joys, their suffering—and was never sated. Just as a man, tormented by hunger, goes to sleep in exhaustion and dreams of sumptuous dishes and sparkling wine before him. He devours the airy gifts of his imagination with rapture, and he feels easier. But as soon as he wakes: the dream disappears . . . and all that remains is hunger and despair redoubled!

And, maybe, I will die tomorrow! . . . And not one being on this earth will have ever understood me totally. Some thought of me as worse, some as better, than I actually am . . . Some will say "he was a good fellow," others will say I was a swine. Both one and the other would be wrong. Given this, does it seem worth the effort to live? And yet, you live, out of curiosity, always wanting something new . . . Amusing and vexing!

It is already a month and a half now since I arrived at Fortress N——. Maxim Maximych has gone hunting . . . I am alone. I am sitting at the window. Gray storm clouds have covered the mountains down to their foothills. The sun, through the mist, looks like a yellow stain. It's cold. The wind is whistling and shaking the shutters . . . How boring! I will take up writing my diaries again, which was interrupted by many strange events.

As I re-read this last page: funny! I thought I would die. This was impossible. I had not yet drained the cup of suffering, and now feel that I have a long while still to live.

How clearly and sharply these past events flood back to my memory! Not one line, not one hue, has been wiped away by time!

I remember that for the duration of the night preceding the duel, I didn't sleep a minute. I couldn't write for long: a mysterious anxiety possessed me. For an hour I walked around my room, then I sat down and opened the novel by Walter Scott that had been lying on the table. Since it was *Old Mortality*, I read it at the start with strain, and then I sank into reveries, carried away by the magical flight of imagination . . . Do they recompense the Scottish bard in the next world for each gratifying minute that his book gives?

Finally the day dawned. My nerves had become calm. I looked at myself in the mirror: a dull pallor had spread over my face, preserving the traces of agonizing insomnia. But my eyes, though encircled with brown shadows, shone proudly and inexorably. I remained content with myself.

Having ordered the horses to be saddled, I dressed and ran down to the bathhouse. Plunging into the cold bubblings of the Narzan, I felt my bodily and spiritual strengths returning. I left the baths fresh and bright, as though I were preparing for a ball. Tell me that the soul and body aren't connected after that!

Returning, I found the doctor at my quarters. He was wearing gray riding breeches, an *arkhaluk*,[20] and a Circassian hat. I started roaring with laughter upon seeing this small figure under an enormous shaggy hat: his face was not at all bellicose and, at that moment in time, it was even longer than usual.

"What makes you so sad, doctor?" I said to him. "Haven't you led people a hundred times to the next world with supreme indifference? Imagine that I have a bilious fever. I may recover, I may die. Either would be according to the order of things. Try to look at me as if I were a patient, afflicted by an illness that is unknown to you—and then your curiosity will be aroused to the highest degree. You can make some important physiological observations of me . . . Is not the expectation of a violent death a genuine illness in fact?"

This thought struck the doctor, and he cheered up.

We mounted our horses. Werner seized the reins with both hands, and we set off. In an instant we galloped past the fortress, through the *slobodka,* and entered the gully; the road twisted along it, half-overgrown with high grasses, intersecting constantly with a noisy stream, across which we had to ford frequently, to the great despair of the doctor, because each time we did his horse stopped in the water.

I don't remember a morning more blue and fresh! The sun had barely appeared from behind the green heights, and the confluence of the heat of its rays and the dying chill of night brought feelings of a sort of sweet anguish to everything. The young day had not yet sent one joyful ray into the gully. But it gilded the summits of the crags hanging over us on either side. The thick-leaved bushes, growing in their deep cracks, showered us with silver rain at the least breath of wind. I remember, at this point, I felt a love for nature greater than at any time before. How interesting to watch a single dewdrop, quivering on a wide vine-leaf and reflecting millions of rainbow rays! How greedily my gaze sought to penetrate the foggy distance! There the path became narrower all the time, the crags bluer and more fearsome, and, finally, it seemed that they converged into an impenetrable wall. We rode in silence.

"Have you written your will?" Werner suddenly asked.

"No."

"And in the case of your death?"

"My beneficiaries will appear by themselves."

"Surely you have friends to whom you would like to send a final farewell?"

I shook my head.

"Surely there is one woman in the world to whom you might like to leave something for memory's sake?"

"Would you like, doctor," I replied to him, "that I bare my soul to you? . . . You see, I have grown out of the times when a person dies, pronouncing the name of their beloved, and bequeathing to their friend a lock of their pomaded or unpomaded hair. Considering near and possible death, I think only about myself—some don't even do that. The friends who will tomorrow forget me, or, worse, those who will pin God knows what cock-and-bull stories on me, and the women who, embracing another, will laugh at me, in order not to arouse jealousy toward the deceased—good luck to them! I have carried only a few ideas out of life's storm—and not one feeling. I have long lived according to the head, not the heart. I consider and analyze my personal passions and actions with a strict curiosity, but without sympathy. There are two people within me: one who lives in the full sense of the word, and the other who reasons and judges him. The first, maybe, in an hour's time may bid forevermore farewell to you and the world, and the second . . . the second? Look doctor: do you see there on that precipice, to the right, three figures blackening the landscape? They are our adversaries I suppose?"

We set off at a trot.

At the foot of the rock-face, in the bushes, three horses were tied up. We tied ours there too, and clambered up the narrow footpath to the little platform, where we were awaited by Grushnitsky, the dragoon captain, and his other second called Ivan Ignatievitch (I have never heard his last name).

"We have been expecting you for a long time," said the dragoon captain with an ironic smile.

I pulled out my timepiece and showed it to him.

He apologized, saying that his watch was running fast.

An embarrassing silence endured for several minutes. Finally the doctor broke it, addressing himself to Grushnitsky.

"It seems to me," he said, "that, having both demonstrated a readiness to fight and having paid these debts to the conditions of honor, you could both, gentlemen, make yourselves understood now and end this matter amicably."

"I am willing," I said.

The captain winked at Grushnitsky, and the latter, thinking I was being a coward, assumed a proud air, though until this minute a dull pallor had spread over his cheeks. For the first time since we arrived, he raised his eyes to me. But there was some sort of unrest in his gaze, indicating an inner struggle.

"Clarify your conditions," he said, "and I will do everything that I can for you, you may rest assured . . ."

"Here are my conditions: that you now publicly retract your slander and ask my forgiveness . . ."

"Gracious sir, I am astonished that you deign to propose such things to me."

"What could I propose to you otherwise?"

"We will shoot . . ."

I shrugged my shoulders.

"As you please, only remember that one of us will certainly be killed."

"Would that it were you . . ."

"And I feel assured of the opposite . . ."

He became embarrassed, turned red, then laughed forcedly.

The captain took him by the arm and led him off to the side. They whispered for a long time. I had arrived in a rather peaceable mood, but all this was starting to madden me.

The doctor walked up to me.

"Listen," he said with evident anxiety. "I suppose you have forgotten about their plot? . . . I don't know how to load a pistol, but if it comes to that . . . You are a strange man! Tell them that you know their intentions, and they won't dare . . . What is this—hunting? They'll shoot you like a bird . . ."

"Please, don't worry, doctor, and wait . . . I will arrange it all so that there is no advantage to their side. Let them whisper . . ."

"Gentlemen, this is getting tiresome!" I said to them loudly. "If we're going to fight then let's fight. You had time yesterday to discuss the matter in its entirety."

"We are ready," the captain answered.

"Take your positions, gentlemen! . . . Doctor, measure six paces, if you please."

"Take your positions!" repeated Ivan Ignatievitch in a squeaky voice.

"Allow me!" I said, ". . . one more condition. Since we are fighting to the death, then we are obliged to do everything possible to make sure that this remains secret and that our seconds aren't held responsible. Do you all agree?"

"Absolutely agreed."

"So, this is what I have devised. Do you see, at the top of that sheer rock-face on the right, there is a narrow platform? From there to the bottom would be about thirty *sazhens,* if not more. Below, there are sharp rocks. Each of us will stand at the edge of the platform—this way, even a light wound will be fatal. This should complement your wishes, since you yourselves set six paces. Whoever is wounded will fly to the bottom without fail and will smash into smithereens. The doctor will extract the bullet, and then this sudden death can be easily explained by an unfortunate leap. We will cast lots to decide who shoots first. I inform you of my inference that I won't otherwise fight."

"As you please!" said the dragoon captain, having looked over at Grushnitsky expressively, who himself nodded his head as a sign of agreement. His face was changing by the minute. I had put him in a difficult situation. Shooting under the usual conditions, he could have aimed at my leg and lightly wounded me, and satisfied his revenge in this way without burdening his conscience too much. But now, he had to shoot at the air, or commit murder, or, finally, abandon his vile scheme and be subjected to an equal danger to mine. At that moment, I wouldn't have wished to be in his place. He led the captain aside and started to talk to him about something with great heat. I saw how his lips were turning blue and trembling. But the captain turned away from him with a contemptuous smile. "You are a fool!" he said to Grushnitsky rather loudly. "You don't understand anything! Let us be off gentlemen!"

The narrow path led between bushes on the slope; the loose steps of this natural staircase were made up of debris from the rock face; hanging on to the shrubs, we started to clamber up. Grushnitsky walked at the front, his seconds behind him, and then the doctor and me.

"You surprise me," said the doctor, taking me firmly by the hand. "Let me take your pulse! . . . Oho! A fever! . . . But nothing is evident from the face . . . only your eyes are shining more brightly than usual."

Suddenly, small rocks started noisily rolling down toward our feet. What was this? The branch that Grushnitsky had been holding onto had snapped; he slipped, and he would have slid down to the bottom on his back, had his seconds not held him up.

"Be careful!" I cried to him. "Don't fall before it's time—it's a bad omen. Remember Julius Caesar!"

We had just climbed to the top of the bluff. The little platform was covered with a fine sand, as though designed for the purposes of a duel. The mountain summits clustered like an innumerable flock all around us, disappearing in the golden clouds of the morning; the white bulk of Elbrus rose up in the south, a lock in the chain of icy pinnacles; stringy clouds, racing in from the east, wandered among the peaks. I went up to the edge of the little platform, looked down, and my head was almost spinning—it looked cold and dark down there, like a grave. The mossy jagged edges of rock, scattered by thunderstorm and time, were awaiting their spoils.

The little platform on which we were meant to fight made a nearly perfect triangle. They measured six paces from the protruding corner and decided that the first of us to whom it would come to face unfriendly fire would stand in that corner, with his back to the edge. If he wasn't killed then the opponents would switch places.

I had decided to give Grushnitsky every advantage. I wanted to test him. Perhaps a spark of magnanimity would be awakened in his soul, and then everything would turn out for the best; but vanity and weakness of character were to be victorious . . . I wanted to give myself full rights to have no mercy on him, if fate would pardon me. Who hasn't negotiated such conditions with their conscience?

"Cast lots, Doctor!" said the captain.

The doctor pulled a silver coin out of his pocket and held it up.

"Tails!" cried Grushnitsky, hurriedly, like a man who has been suddenly wakened by a friendly nudge.

"Heads!" I said.

The coin soared up and fell ringing. Everyone rushed toward it.

"You are lucky," I said to Grushnitsky. "You shoot first! But remember that if you don't kill me, then I won't miss. I give you my honest word."

He blushed. He was ashamed to kill an unarmed man. I looked at him intently. For about a minute it seemed to me that he would throw himself at my feet, begging forgiveness. But how could you admit to such a vile scheme? One means remained for him—to shoot into the air. I was sure that he would shoot into the air! Just one thing could prevent this: the thought that I would request a second duel.

"It's time," the doctor whispered to me, tugging me by the sleeve. "If you don't now say that we know their intentions, then everything is lost. Look, he is already loading . . . if you don't say something then I will . . ."

"Not for anything in the world, doctor!" I answered, holding him back by the arm. "You will ruin everything. You gave me your word that you wouldn't get in my way . . . What is it to you? Perhaps I want to be killed . . ."

He looked at me in surprise.

"Oh, that is another matter! . . . Only don't complain about me in the next world . . ."

Meanwhile the captain was loading his pistols; he handed one to Grushnitsky, whispering something to him with a little smile; and handed the other to me.

I stood in the corner of the little platform, having tightly wedged my left foot against a rock and leaning a little forward so that in the event of a light wound I would not topple backward.

Grushnitsky stood opposite me, and when given the signal he began to raise his pistol. His knees were shaking. He aimed straight at my forehead . . .

An indescribable rage started boiling in my breast.

Suddenly he lowered the muzzle of the pistol and, turning pale as a sheet, turned to his second.

"I can't," he said in a dull voice.

"Coward!" the captain responded.

A shot rang out. The bullet scratched my knee. I couldn't help taking a few steps forward, to move away from the edge as soon as possible.

"Well, brother Grushnitsky, too bad that you missed!"

said the captain. "Now it's your turn: take up your position! Embrace me first: we won't see each other again!"

They embraced; the captain could barely keep himself from laughing. "Don't be afraid," he added, slyly looking at Grushnitsky. "Everything on earth is nonsense! . . . Nature is a fool, fate is a turkey, and life is a *kopeck*!"

With this tragic phrase, delivered with decorous importance, he walked to his place. Grushnitsky was then also embraced by a teary-eyed Ivan Ignatievitch and then remained alone before me. I am still trying to explain to myself what kind of feeling was agitating then in my breast: it was the vexation of insulted vanity, and contempt, and anger, borne of the thought that this man, looking at me now with such assurance, with such calm impertinence, had, but two minutes ago, without exposing himself to any danger, wanted to kill me like a dog, for if he had wounded me a little more forcefully, I would have definitely fallen from the crag.

I looked him intently in the face for several minutes, trying to note at least a faint trace of repentance. But it seemed to me that he was holding back a smile.

"I advise you to pray to God before you die," I said to him then.

"Don't worry more about my soul than your own. Just one thing I'll ask of you: fire sooner."

"And you don't retract your slander? You won't ask my forgiveness? . . . Think now, isn't your conscience telling you something?"

"Mr. Pechorin!" cried the dragoon captain. "You are not here to hear a confession, allow me to remark . . . Let us be done with this. Suppose someone were to pass through the gully—and were to see us."

"Very good, doctor, come here."

The doctor approached. The poor doctor! He was paler than Grushnitsky had been ten or so minutes ago.

I pronounced the following words purposefully, with pauses, loudly and distinctly, just as they pronounce death sentences:

"Doctor, these gentlemen, likely in haste, have forgotten to put a bullet in my pistol. I ask you to load it again—and well!"

"It's not possible!" cried the captain. "It's not possible! I loaded both pistols. Unless, perhaps the ball rolled out of yours . . . and that's not my fault! But you don't have the right to reload . . . no right . . . this is completely against the rules, and I don't allow it . . ."

"Good!" I said to the captain, "if that is so, then you and I will shoot under the very same conditions . . ." He stopped short.

Grushnitsky stood, having lowered his head onto his breast, embarrassed and dismal.

"Let them!" he said finally to the captain, who wanted to pull my pistol from the doctor's hands . . . "You know yourself that they are right."

In vain, the captain was making various signals to him—and Grushnitsky didn't want to look.

In the meantime, the doctor had loaded the pistol and given it to me. Having seen this, the captain spat and stamped his foot.

"You are such a fool, brother," he said. "A vulgar fool! . . . Since you put yourself in my hands you should listen to me in everything . . . It serves you right! Die, like a fly . . ."

He turned and walked off, muttering, "And anyway, this is completely against the rules."

"Grushnitsky!" I said. "There is still time. Retract your slander, and I will forgive you everything. You didn't succeed in fooling me, and my vanity is satisfied—remember, we were once friends . . ."

His face flared up, his eyes sparkled.

"Shoot!" he answered. "I despise myself, and I hate you. If you don't kill me, I will stab you from around a corner one night. There isn't room on this earth for both of us . . ."

I shot . . .

When the smoke had dissipated, there was no Grushnitsky on the platform. Only a light pillar of dust still curled up at the edge of the precipice.

Everyone cried out in one voice.

"*É finita la commedia!*"[21] I said to the doctor.

He didn't reply and turned away in horror.

I shrugged my shoulders and exchanged bows with Grushnitsky's seconds.

Going down the path, I noticed Grushnitsky's bloody corpse between fissures in the rock. I couldn't help closing my eyes . . . Leading my horse away, I set off for home at a walking pace. There was a stone in my heart. The sun seemed dim to me, its rays didn't warm me.

Before reaching the *slobodka,* I turned right along the gully. The sight of another person would have been distressing to me. I wanted to be alone. Having let go of the reins and lowered my head onto my breast, I rode for a long time, and finally found myself in a place that was entirely unknown to me. I turned the horse around and started to search for the road. The sun was already setting when I rode up toward Kislovodsk, worn out, on a worn-out horse.

My lackey told me that Werner had come by and delivered two notes. One from him, the other . . . from Vera.

I unsealed the first, and it had the following contents:

Everything was arranged as best as it could have been. The body has been brought back, disfigured, the bullet pulled from its breast. Everyone is convinced that the cause of his death was an unfortunate accident. The commandant, to whom our disagreement is probably known, only shook his head but didn't say anything. There is no evidence of any kind against you, and you can sleep peacefully . . . If you are able . . . Farewell . . .

I took a long time in deciding to open the second note . . . What could she have written to me? . . . A heavy foreboding worried my soul.

This is it, the letter, of which each word is indelibly marked onto my memory:

I am writing to you in the full certainty that we will never see each other again. I thought the same several years or so ago upon parting ways with you. But it pleased the heavens to test me a second time. I didn't withstand this test—my weak heart submitted again to that familiar voice ... you won't despise me for this, isn't that true? This letter will take the place of a farewell and a confession: I am obliged to tell you everything that has accumulated in my heart since the moment it started loving you. I won't begin by accusing you. You have behaved with me as any other man would have behaved with me. You loved me as property, as a source of joy, anxiety, and sadness, all mutually exchangeable, without which life is tedious and monotonous. I understood this at the beginning. But you were unhappy and I sacrificed myself, hoping that at some point you would value my sacrifice, that at some point you would understand my profound affection, which didn't come with any conditions. Much time has passed since then. I penetrated every secret of your soul ... and became convinced that it had been a useless aspiration. How bitter it was for me! But my love had grown into my soul. It had dimmed but it had not gone out.

We are parting forever. However, you can be sure that I will never love another. My soul spent all of its treasures on you, its tears and its hopes too. Having once loved you, it is impossible for me to look at other men without a certain contempt—not because you are better than them—oh no! But there is something in your nature that is special, that belongs to you alone, something proud and mysterious. In your voice, no matter what you have said, there is an invincible power. No one is capable of wanting to be loved as much as you. Evil is not as attractive in anyone but you, no one's gaze promises as much bliss, no one is able to use their advantages better, and no one can be as sincerely unhappy as you, because no one strives as much to convince himself of the contrary.

Now I should explain to you the reason for my hasty departure. It will seem of little importance to you, because it affects me alone.

This morning, my husband came to me and told me about your disagreement with Grushnitsky. Evidently, my face changed very much, because he looked me in the eyes, long and hard. I nearly fainted at the thought that you were to fight today and that I was the reason for it. It seemed to me that I would go mad . . . but now that I can reason, I am sure that you will remain alive. It is impossible that you would die without me, impossible! My husband paced the room for a long time. I don't know what he was saying to me, I don't remember what I was saying in reply . . . I probably told him that I love you . . . I only remember that near the end of our conversation, he insulted me with the most terrible words and left. I listened as he ordered the carriage to be harnessed . . . And here it is already three o'clock as I sit at the window and wait for your return . . . But you are alive—you cannot die! . . . The carriage is almost ready . . . Farewell, farewell . . . I am perished—but what does it matter? . . . If only I could be sure that you will always remember me—I won't speak of love— no, only remembering . . . Farewell. They're coming . . . I must hide this letter . . .

Is it true that you are not in love with Mary? You won't marry her? Listen, you must do this for me as a sacrifice: I have lost everything in this world to you . . .

Like a lunatic, I leapt out onto the veranda and jumped on my Circassian horse, who was being led around the courtyard, and set off at full tilt along the road to Pyatigorsk. I spurred the worn-out horse mercilessly onward, and he rushed me along the rocky road, snorting and covered with foam.

The sun had already concealed itself in the black clouds that were resting on the ridge of the western mountains. It was becoming dark and damp in the gully. The Podkumok River forced its way through the rocks, bellowing darkly and monotonously. I rode at a furious pace, gasping for breath out of impatience. The thought of not finding her in Pyatigorsk was beating me like a hammer on the heart!

One minute, just to see her for one more minute, to bid farewell, to squeeze her hand . . . I prayed, I cursed, I wept, I laughed . . . No, nothing could express my troubled mind, my desperation! . . . Before the possibility of losing her forever, Vera became dearer to me than everything in the world—dearer than life itself, than honor, than happiness! God knows what peculiar, what mad ideas swarmed in my head . . . And meanwhile, I continued to ride at a furious pace, spurring my horse mercilessly onward. And then I started to notice that my horse was breathing more heavily. He had already stumbled twice on even ground . . . There were five *verst*s more to Essentukov—a Cossack station, where I could exchange my horse.

All would have been saved had my horse had enough strength for another ten minutes! But suddenly, passing up out of a small gully, at an egress from the mountains, on a tight bend, he crashed to the ground. I swiftly jumped off— at this point I wanted to get him up and was holding the reins—all in vain. A faint moan escaped from between his clenched teeth; after a few minutes, he expired. I was left alone on the Steppe, having lost my last hope. I tried to continue on foot; my legs gave way, exhausted with the distress of the day and insomnia, then I fell onto the wet grass and cried like an infant.

For a long time I lay motionless and wept bitterly, not making any attempt to restrain my tears and sobbing. I thought that my breast would explode. All my hardness, all my cool indifference, disappeared like smoke. My soul lost its strength, my reason went quiet, and if someone had seen me at that minute, they would have turned away in disdain.

When the dew of night and the mountain wind had refreshed my hot head, and my thoughts had returned to regular order, I understood that chasing after a perished happiness was useless and heedless. What did I need? To see her? Why? Had not everything ended between us? One bitter departing kiss wouldn't distill my memories, and would only make it harder to part ways thereafter.

It was pleasant, to me, however, that I could cry! As for the rest, it may be that the cause of this was shattered nerves, a night without sleep, two minutes in the face of a pistol's muzzle, and an empty stomach.

All will be better! This new suffering, to use a military idiom, has given me a fortunate diversion. Weeping is healthy. And moreover, it is likely that, had I not set off on horseback, and not been made to walk fifteen *versts* back, then sleep wouldn't have closed my eyes that night.

I returned to Kislovodsk at five o'clock in the morning, threw myself on my bed, and slept the sleep of Napoleon after Waterloo.

When I wakened, it was already dark in the courtyard. I sat by the open window, unbuttoned my *arkhaluk,* and the mountain wind refreshed my breast, which had still not calmed with the heavy sleep of fatigue. The lights of the fortress and the *slobodka* twinkled in the distance, beyond the river, through the tops of the thick linden trees that overshadowed it. All was quiet in our courtyard; it was dark in the house of the Princess Ligovsky.

The doctor came by. His brow was crossed, and he did not extend his hand to me as he would usually.

"Where have you come from, Doctor?"

"From the Princess Ligovsky. Her daughter is ill—with a weakening of the nerves . . . But that is not the matter, this is: the town authorities have guessed the truth, even though they can't positively prove anything. However, I advise you to be more careful. The Princess Ligovsky was telling me today that she knows that you dueled for her daughter's sake. That little old man told her everything . . . what was his name? He was witness to your skirmish with Grushnitsky in the restaurant. I have come to warn you. Farewell. It may be that we will never see each other again, that they will dispatch you somewhere."

He stopped at the threshold. He wanted to shake my hand . . . and if I had given him the slightest indication of such a desire on my part, he would have thrown his arms around my neck. But I stayed cold, like a rock—and he walked out.

People! They are all the same: they know all the bad aspects to a deed in advance, and they help you, advise you, even approve of it, seeing that no other way is possible—and then they wash their hands of it and turn away with indignation from the person who had the courage to take the whole burden of responsibility onto himself. They are all the same, even the kindest, the most intelligent of them!

The next morning, having received an order from the authorities to take myself to the Fortress N——, I went to the Princess Ligovsky to bid them farewell.

She was astonished when, to her question of whether I had something especially important to say to her, I replied that I wished her happiness, et cetera.

"Well, I need to speak with you about something very serious."

I sat down, saying nothing.

It was obvious that she didn't know how to begin. Her face turned crimson, her plump fingers tapped the table. Finally she started like this, in a broken voice:

"Listen, Monsieur Pechorin! I think that you are a noble man."

I bowed.

"Indeed I am convinced of it," she continued, "though your behavior has been somewhat dubious. But you may have your reasons, which I don't know, and you must now confide them to me. You defended my daughter from slander, you dueled for her sake—which is to say that you risked your life for her . . . Don't say anything, I know that you won't admit to it, because Grushnitsky is killed (she made the sign of the cross). God will forgive him—and, I hope He will forgive you too! . . . But this is not my concern, I cannot judge you because my daughter, though she was innocent, was nonetheless the cause of it. She told me everything . . . I think it was everything. You declared your love for her . . . she confessed hers to you (here the princess exhaled heavily). But she is ill, and I am sure that this is not a simple illness! A secret sadness is killing her. She doesn't admit to it, but I am sure that you are the cause of it . . . Listen, you may think that I am seeking an official with enormous wealth for her—disabuse yourself! I only want the happiness of my daughter. Your current situation is unenviable, but it can be righted. You have means. My daughter loves you, she is brought up to make a husband happy. I am wealthy, and she is my only child . . . Tell me, what is holding you back? You see, I wasn't supposed to tell you all of this, but I count upon your heart, upon your honor. Remember that I have only one daughter . . . only one . . ."

She started to weep.

"Princess," I said. "It is impossible for me to answer you. Allow me please to speak with your daughter alone . . ."

"Never!" she exclaimed, getting up from her chair with great emotion.

"As you wish," I replied, preparing myself to leave.

She became distracted, gestured to me with her hand that I should wait, and went out.

About five minutes passed. My heart was pounding, but my thoughts were calm, my head was cold. As much as I tried to find a spark of love in my heart toward the lovely Mary, my strivings were in vain.

Then the doors opened, and she came in. Good God! How she had changed since I had last seen her—was it that long ago?

Walking to the middle of the room, she swayed. I jumped up, gave her my arm, and led her to an armchair.

I stood opposite her. We were silent for a long time. Her big eyes, filled with indescribable sorrow it seemed, were looking into mine with something resembling hope. Her pale lips tried to smile in vain. Her delicate hands, crossed on her knees, were so thin and transparent that I felt pity for her.

"Princess," I said, "did you know that I was mocking you? . . . You should despise me."

A sickly flush appeared in her cheeks.

I continued, "Therefore, you cannot love me . . ."

She turned away, leaned her elbows on the table, and covered her eyes with her hand, and it seemed to me that they glistened with tears.

"My God!" she uttered, barely distinguishably.

This was becoming unbearable—in a minute I would fall to her feet.

"So, as you can see yourself," I said, with as firm a voice as I could, and a forced grin, "you can see for yourself that I cannot marry you; even if you might want this right now, you would soon rue it. My conversation with your mama has forced me to clarify this so plainly and grossly. I hope that she is in error. It will be easy for you to persuade her to the contrary. You see, in your eyes, I am playing the most pitiful and vile role, and I am even admitting to it. This is all I can do for you. Whatever bad opinion you hold of me, I submit to it . . . You see, I am lowly before you. Isn't it true that even if at one time you loved me, that from this minute you despise me?"

She turned to me, pale as marble—only her eyes sparkled marvelously.

"I hate you," she said.

I thanked her, bowed politely, and left.

An hour later, a courier *troika* was rushing me from Kislovodsk. A few *verst*s from Essentukov I recognized the corpse of my spirited horse near the road. The saddle was removed—probably by passing Cossacks—and instead of the saddle, on his back stood two crows. I exhaled and turned away . . .

And now, here, in this boring fortress, I often ask myself, running through thoughts of the past: why didn't I want to follow the path opened to me by fate, where quiet happiness and spiritual peace awaited me? . . . No, such a fate wouldn't have agreed with me! I am like a sailor, born and bred on the deck of a pirate ship. His soul has got used to storms and battles, and, when thrown ashore, he pines and languishes much as the shady groves beckon him, much as the peaceful sun shines at him. He walks along the coastal sands all day, listening to the monotonous murmur of the lapping waves and peering into the cloudy distance: is that the sail he seeks, on the pale line that separates the blue deep from the little gray storm clouds—at first resembling the wing of a seagull, but little by little, separating from the foam of the boulders, with a steady approach toward the deserted jetty . . .

3
THE FATALIST

I once happened to spend two weeks in a Cossack *stanitsa*[1] on the left flank. An infantry battalion was stationed there. The officers gathered in one another's quarters in turns, and played cards.

Once, we stayed up late at Major S——'s, having become bored with Boston[2] and thrown the cards under the table. The conversation was, for once, entertaining. We were discussing the Muslim belief that apparently says the fate of a man is written in the sky; this also finds many believers among us Christians. Each of us was recounting various unusual occurrences, *pro* and *contra*.

"All this, gentlemen, doesn't prove anything," said the old major. "Indeed, none of you have borne witness to these strange occurrences with which you are shoring up your opinions."

"None of us has, of course," the men said, "but we have heard these things from trusted people . . ."

"All this is nonsense!" someone said. "Where are these trusted people, who have seen this list that tells us the appointed hour of our death? . . . And if there is definitely such thing as predestination—why were we given free will, and reason? Why should we atone for our actions?"

At this time, an officer who had been sitting in the corner of the room stood and walked slowly up to the table, throwing a cool glance at the company. He was a Serbian type, which was evident from his name.

The exterior of Lieutenant Vulich corresponded entirely with his character. His great height and the dark complexion of his face, his black hair, his black and penetrating eyes, a big but straight nose (characteristic of his nation), a sad and cold smile eternally roaming on his lips—all this seemed to coordinate itself in giving him the look of a special being, not able to share thoughts and passions with those whom fate had given him to be his comrades.

He was brave, spoke little but incisively; he did not entrust anyone with the secrets of his spirit or family. He hardly drank wine, never pursued young Cossack girls—the charms of whom it is difficult to imagine without seeing them. They used to say, however, that the wife of the colonel was not indifferent to his expressive eyes. But he became seriously angry when you hinted at this.

There was only one passion that he didn't hide: a passion for gambling. At the green table he forgot everything, and usually lost. But constant losses only aggravated his stubborn nature. They say that once, during a night expedition, he was keeping bank on his pillow, and he was having terrific luck. Suddenly shots rang out, an alarm was raised, everyone jumped up and dashed to their guns.

"Stake the bank!" cried Vulich to one of the hottest betters, without getting up.

"Sevens," replied the other, running off. Disregarding the general chaos, Vulich shuffled the double-deck of cards, and the card was dealt.

When he appeared on the front line, there was already a fierce gunfight in progress. Vulich didn't bother himself about the bullets, or the Chechen sabers. He was looking for his lucky punter.

"Seven it is!" he cried, finding him at last in the line of skirmishers, which had started to force the enemy out of the forest. Walking closer, he pulled out his coin-purse and wallet and gave them both to the lucky man, not paying attention to objections about the inappropriateness of the payment. Having fulfilled this unpleasant debt, he threw himself forward, carrying the soldiers along and fired back and forth with the Chechens with a cold and calm head, until the end.

When Lieutenant Vulich walked up to the table, everyone fell silent, expecting some original trick from him.

"Gentlemen!" he said (his voice was calm, even though his tone was lower than usual). "Gentlemen! What is this empty argument? You want proof: I suggest you put this to the test yourselves. Perhaps there is a person who will exercise his will and put their life at our disposal, or is a fateful minute affixed to each of us beforehand . . . Who is game?"

"Not me, not me," resounded from every side. "What a crank! The things that enter his head!"

"I'll make a wager!" I said, joking.

"Which one?"

"I assert that predestination does not exist," I said, pouring some two dozen gold pieces onto the table—everything that was in my pocket.

"I'll take it," replied Vulich in a muffled voice. "Major, you will be the judge; here are fifteen gold pieces, the remaining five you owe me, and please do me the kindness of adding them to this."

"I will," said the major, "only I don't understand, really, what is happening, and how you will decide the matter?"

Vulich went into the major's sleeping quarters without saying anything; we followed him. He walked up to a wall where some guns were hanging. At random he took down one of the variously calibered pistols from its nail; we still didn't understand him but when he cocked the gun and poured gunpowder into the pan, many couldn't help but cry out, and they grabbed his arms.

"What do you want to do? Listen, this is madness!" they screamed at him.

"Gentlemen!" he said slowly, freeing his hands. "Whom would it please to pay twenty gold pieces on my behalf?"

Everyone went quiet and stepped away.

Vulich walked into the other room and sat at the table. Everyone followed him. With a gesture, he invited us to sit down in a circle. Silently we obeyed him. At that moment he had acquired some kind of secret power over us. I looked him intently in the eye. With a calm and motionless gaze, he met my searching look, and his pale lips smiled. But, despite his composure, it seemed to me that I could read the stamp of death on his pale face. I had been making observations, and many old soldiers had confirmed my observations, that there is often some sort of strange imprint of inescapable fate on the face of a man who would die in a few hours' time, so much so that to an experienced eye it is hard to mistake.

"You will die today!" I said to him.

He turned quickly to me, but answered slowly and calmly:

"Maybe yes, maybe no . . ." And then, addressing the major, he asked, "Is the pistol loaded?" The major in confusion couldn't remember very well.

"Yes, it is, Vulich!" someone cried. "Of course it's loaded if it's hanging at the head of the bed—why play the fool?"

"A stupid joke!" another chimed in.

"I'll wager fifty rubles to five that the pistol isn't loaded!" a third cried out.

New bets were made.

I was becoming fed up with this long ceremony.

"Listen," I said, "either shoot yourself or hang the pistol back in its former place and let's all go to bed."

"Of course," many exclaimed, "let's all go to bed."

"Gentlemen, I ask you to not move from your places!" said Vulich, putting the muzzle of the pistol to his forehead. Everyone seemed to turn to stone.

"Mr. Pechorin," he added, "take a card and throw it up."

I took, as I remember it now, an ace of hearts from the table and threw it upward; everyone's breathing stopped; all eyes, showing fear and a sort of ambiguous curiosity, ran between the pistol and the fateful ace, which quivered in the air and slowly fell. The moment it touched the table, Vulich pulled the trigger . . . a misfire!

"Thank God!" many cried out. "It wasn't loaded!"

"But, let's see . . ." said Vulich. He cocked the gun again and took aim at a military cap hanging above the window. A shot rang out—the smoke filled the room. When it dissipated, they took down the military cap: it was shot right through the middle, and the bullet was lodged deeply in the wall.

About three minutes passed, and no one could utter a word. Vulich poured my gold pieces into his purse.

There was talk about the fact that the pistol didn't fire the first time; some maintained that the pan had probably been clogged, others were saying in whispers that the gunpowder was damp the first time and that Vulich had poured some fresh powder into it afterward. But I claimed that the latter suggestion was unfounded, because I hadn't taken my eyes from the pistol once.

"You are lucky in gambling," I said to Vulich.

"For the first time since I was born," he replied, smiling with self-satisfaction. "This is better than faro[3] and stuss."[4]

"And a little more dangerous, too."

"What's this? Are you starting to believe in pre-destination?"

"I believe in it; but I don't understand why I was so certain that you would die today . . ."

And the man, who had aimed so coolly at his own forehead not long ago, now suddenly blushed and became embarrassed.

"Enough now!" he said, standing up. "Our wager has been settled, and now your observations, I think, are inappropriate . . ." He took his hat and walked out. This seemed strange to me—and for good reason!

Soon everyone dispersed to their houses, variously talking about Vulich's caprice and, probably, unanimously calling me an egoist since I had made a wager with a man who wanted to shoot himself. As if, without me, he wouldn't have found a convenient occasion!

I was returning home along the empty lanes of the *stanitsa;* the moon, full and red, like the glow of a fire, was beginning to show itself from behind the jagged horizon of houses. The stars calmly shone in the dark-blue vault of the sky, and I was amused to remember that there were once very sage people who thought that heavenly bodies took part in our insignificant arguments over little tufts of earth or over various invented rights . . . ! And what happened? These lamps which were lit, in their opinion in order to illuminate their battles and victories, still burn with their original brilliance, while their own passions and hopes were extinguished long ago along with their very selves, like small fires lit at the edge of a wood by a careless wanderer! And then what force of will gave them the conviction that the whole sky, with its innumerable population, was watching them with constant concern, mute though it may have been! . . . And we, their pitiful descendants, wandering the earth without conviction or pride, without pleasure or fear, but with that involuntary dread that grips the heart at the thought of an inescapable end—we are no longer able to be great martyrs, not for the good of mankind, nor even for the sake of our own happiness, because we know it is impossible. And we shift indifferently from one doubt to another, just as our ancestors rushed from one delusion to the next, but without having, as they did, either hope or even that indeterminate but real pleasure that meets the soul in every struggle with people or fate . . .

Many similar such thoughts passed through my mind, and I didn't suppress them because I don't like to dwell on any sort of abstract thought. Where would that lead me? . . . In my early youth I was a dreamer, I loved to cherish gloomy and iridescent images in turn, which my restless and thirsty imagination painted for me. But what did this leave me with? Only fatigue, like that which comes after a nocturnal battle with a specter, and dim recollections, filled with regret. In this pointless struggle I exhausted both the fire of my soul and the constancy of my will, both necessary for a real life. I then set about living this life, having survived it already in my thoughts, and I became bored and repulsed, like a man who is reading a stupid imitation of a book with which he has long been familiar.

The incidents of the evening had made a rather deep impression on me and agitated my nerves. I do not know whether now I do indeed believe in predestination or not, but I firmly believed in it that night. The proof was striking, and despite the fact that I had mocked our ancestors and their obliging astrology, I had fallen involuntarily into their trap but stopped myself from following this dangerous path just in time. And having the rule of never rejecting anything absolutely, and never believing in anything blindly, I threw out metaphysics and started to look beneath my feet. Such precaution was very apt. I nearly fell, stumbling on something fat and soft, but by all appearances, not living. I stooped—the moon was shining directly onto the road—and what was it? In front of me lay a swine, cleaved in half by a saber . . . I had barely managed to examine it when I heard the noise of footsteps. Two Cossacks were running from the alley; one walked up to me and asked if I had seen a drunk Cossack chasing a swine. I declared to them that I had not met said Cossack and pointed to the unfortunate victim of his frenzied bravery.

"What a scoundrel!" said the second Cossack. "When he drinks too much *chikhir*,[5] then he's off hacking to pieces everything that he sees. Let's go after him, Yeremeich, we must tie him up, otherwise . . ."

They went off, and I continued on my path with great care and happily made it to my quarters at last.

I stayed with an old *uryadnik*,[6] whom I loved for his good morals, and especially for his pretty daughter, Nastya.

She was waiting for me at the wicket gate as usual, wrapped in a fur coat. The moon lit up her lovely lips, which had turned a little blue from the cold of the night. Having recognized me, she smiled, but I wasn't in the mood. "Good night, Nastya," I said, walking past. She wanted to say something in reply but simply sighed.

I closed the door to my room behind me and lit the candle and fell onto my bed. But slumber made me wait for it longer than usual. The east was already paling when I fell asleep, but apparently it was written in the skies that I wouldn't get a good night's sleep. At four o'clock in the morning, two fists knocked on my window. I jumped up. "What is it?"

"Get up! Get dressed!" various voices cried to me. I quickly dressed and went out. "Do you know what has happened?" three officers asked me in unison, coming for me. They were as pale as death.

"What?"

"Vulich has been killed."

I turned to stone.

"Yes, killed," they continued. "Let's go, quickly."

"Where to?!"

"You'll find out on the way . . ."

We went off. They told me all that had happened, adding remarks about the strange predestination that had saved him from inevitable death half an hour before his death. Vulich had been walking alone along a dark street; the drunk Cossack who had cleaved the swine galloped at him and might have passed him by without noticing Vulich had the latter not stopped and said:

"Brother, whom are you looking for?"

"You!" replied the Cossack, striking him with his saber, slicing him from the shoulder almost to the heart . . . The two Cossacks I encountered, who had been tracking the murderer, had appeared just then; they picked up the wounded man, but he was already at his final breath, saying, "He was right!" I alone understood the dark meaning of these words. They referred to me. I had involuntarily predicted his poor fate. My instinct had not fooled me. I had correctly read the stamp of near demise in his altered face.

The murderer had locked himself in an empty hut at the end of the *stanitsa*. We went there. A mass of women were weeping while running in the same direction. From time to time a tardy Cossack galloped out onto the street, hurriedly fastening his dagger to his belt, and outstripping us at a gallop.

The turmoil was terrible.

At long last we arrived. We watched: a crowd stood around the peasant house, the doors and shutters of which were locked from the inside. Officers and Cossacks talked heatedly among themselves. The women were wailing, condemning and reckoning. My eyes were cast on to an old woman among them, whose conspicuous face was expressing mad despair. She was sitting on a thick log, leaning her elbows on her knees, and supporting her head with her hands: it was the mother of the murderer. Her lips stirred from time to time. Were they whispering a curse or a prayer?

In the meantime, something needed to be resolved, and the criminal needed to be captured. No one, however, dared to cast himself forward. I walked up to the window and looked through a chink in the shutters. He lay on the floor, pale, holding a pistol in his right hand. His bloodied saber lay next to him. His expressive eyes were rolling around in a frightening way. Now and then he flinched and grabbed hold of his head, as if indistinctly remembering yesterday's events. I didn't read any significant resolution in this agitated gaze and said to the major that it was pointless of him not to order the Cossacks to break down the door and rush in because it would be better done now than later when he had completely come to his senses.

At this time, old Esaul walked up to the door and called him by name; the latter responded.

"You have sinned, brother Efimych," said Esaul, "and there's nothing to be done—give yourself up!"

"I will not give up!" answered the Cossack.

"Fear God. After all, you are not an accursed Chechen, but an honest Christian. And well, if your sin has led you astray, then there is nothing to be done—you won't avoid your fate!"

"I will not give up!" the Cossack cried threateningly, and the cracking of his cocking-piece was audible.

"Hey, auntie," said Esaul to the old woman, "talk to your boy, perhaps he will listen to you . . . All this will only anger God. Yes, and see here, these men have waited two hours already."

The old woman looked at him intently and shook her head.

"Vasily Petrovich," said Esaul, walking up to the major. "He won't give himself up—I know him. But if we break down the door, then many of our people will be killed. Would it not be better to order him shot? There is a big chink in the shutters."

At that minute a strange thought flashed through my head: like Vulich, I was thinking of testing fate.

"Wait," I said to the major, "I will get him alive."

Having ordered Esaul to engage him in conversation and placing three Cossacks at the door, ready to beat it down and rush to my aid at the given signal, I walked around the peasant house and approached the fateful window. My heart was pounding.

"Oh, you, accursed man!" cried Esaul. "What are you doing—mocking us, are you? Or do you think we won't get the better of you?"

He started knocking on the door with all his might. Having put my eye to the chink in the shutter, I followed the movements of the Cossack, who wasn't expecting an attack from this side. And suddenly I ripped off the shutter and flung myself headfirst through the window. A shot rang out just above my ear; the bullet tore my epaulet. But the smoke that had filled the room prevented my opponent from finding his saber, which was lying next to him. I grabbed him by the arm; the Cossacks burst in, and three minutes hadn't passed before the criminal was tied up and led off under guard. The people walked off. The officers congratulated me—and for good reason!

After all this, how could one not become a fatalist? But who knows for sure if he is convinced of something or not? . . . And how often do we take a deception of feelings or a blunder of common sense for a conviction!

I love to doubt everything: this inclination of mind doesn't hinder the decisiveness of a character—on the contrary, as far as I am concerned, I am always braver going forward when I don't know what to expect. After all, nothing can happen that is worse than death—and you can't avoid death!

Having returned to the fortress, I recounted to Maxim Maximych all that had happened to me and all that I had witnessed, and wanted to know his opinion on the count of predestination. At first he didn't understand the word, but I explained it to him as best I could and then he said significantly, shaking his head:

"Yes, sir. Of course. Quite a wise old joke! . . . But those Asian cocking-pieces frequently misfire if they are badly greased or if you haven't pressed hard enough with your finger. I admit I don't much like Chechen rifles, either. They are somehow unbecoming to our brothers. The butt is small—look into them and you burn your nose! That said, their sabers demand respect, pure and simple!"

Then, having thought for a while, he added:

"Yes, I have pity for the wretch . . . The devil possessed him to talk to a drunk that night! But, clearly, it had been written for him in the sky at his birth . . . !"

I couldn't get any more out of him; he doesn't like metaphysical debates in general.

Notes

FOREWORD

1. Rus': A term referring to an ancient people and their land, which are latterly represented by the Belarusian, Ukrainian, and Russian peoples and their territories.

I. BELA

1. *dukhan:* An inn in the Caucasus.
2. *verst:* An obsolete Russian measurement equal to about 3,500 feet.
3. *troika:* A carriage drawn by three horses harnessed side by side.
4. *saklyas:* Caucasian mountain huts.
5. Lermontov uses the word *burka* here, a felt cloak worn in the Caucasus.
6. *bouza:* A kind of fermented alcohol made from millet.
7. peaceable prince: The term for a local chieftain who took no sides in the war between the Caucasian tribes and the Russians.
8. peaceable prince: A tribal leader who cooperated with Russian forces in the Caucasus.
9. *kunak:* This means true friend, blood brother.
10. *aul:* A Caucasian village.
11. *balalaika:* A Russian stringed instrument with a triangular body and long neck.
12. *dzhigits:* Caucasian horsemen known for equestrian feats and trick-riding.
13. galloon: Braid or lace made of metal, typically used in military uniform.
14. chamois: A goatlike animal native to the Caucasus mountains.

15. *abreks:* A kind of freedom-fighter in the Caucasus. This word is also used to describe bandits and outcasts.
16. *beshmet:* A kind of quilted coat.
17. "Yakshi tkhe, chek yakshi!": This means "A good horse, very good!"
18. *gyaurs:* Non-Muslims. The word is a Turkic version of the Persian word for infidel.
19. Karagyoz: A Turkic name, which literally means "black eyes," but also refers to a Turkish shadow puppet, popular for many centuries in countries near Turkey.
20. *Yok:* This means "no" or "not." It is said to be Tatar.
21. *gurda:* An expensive weapon made of high-quality steel.
22. *Padishah:* This was a title for the Sultan of Turkey.
23. There is a footnote here in Lermontov's original: Я прошу прощения у читателей в том, что переложил в стихи песню Казбича, переданную мне, разумеется, прозой; но привычка—вторая натура. (Прим. Лермонтова.)
24. *yashmak:* A type of Turkish veil worn by women.
25. *Urus—yaman, yaman!:* This means "The Russian is bad, bad!"
26. *peri:* A term of endearment referring to fairylike creatures who are fallen angels.
27. *muzhik:* A male Russian peasant.
28. Russ: An older word meaning "Russian man."
29. *dear little:* this refers to provincial Russian cities and has a slightly pejorative tone (hence the italics, which were in Lermontov's original).
30. Krestovaya: This is a mountain, the name of which translates as "Mountain of the Cross."
31. Nightingale-Robber: A figure from Russian folklore who wrought havoc and was able to render people immobile by whistling.
32. *lezginka:* A folk dance of the Lezgin people.
33. *sazhen:* An obsolete Russian measurement equal to seven feet.
34. *thermalam:* Fabric used for lining, usually linen or cotton.

II. MAXIM MAXIMICH

1. *dolman:* A Hungarian jacket.
2. Balzac's thirty-year-old coquette: This refers to Honoré de Balzac's novel *La Femme de Trente Ans* (1834).

PECHORIN'S DIARIES

FOREWORD

1. Rousseau's confessions: This refers to *Les Confessions* by Rousseau.

1. TAMAN

1. *izba:* A traditional Russian log house.
2. *fatera:* This word means quarters.
3. *slobodka:* A settlement exempted from normal State obligations.
4. On that day the dumb shall cry out: A reference to the Bible, Isaiah 35:5–6: "Then shall the lame man leap as an hart and the tongue of the dumb sing."
5. *uryadnik:* A Cossack NCO, a noncommissioned officer.
6. *rusalka:* A water nymph, frequently demonic, who lives underwater, often at the bottom of rivers.
7. La Jeune-France: A group of young French writers of the 1830s who are known to have exaggerated the theories of Romanticism. They looked up to Victor Hugo.
8. Mignon: A character in Goethe's novel *Wilhelm Meisters Lehrjahre.*

2. PRINCESS MARY

1. The opening line of a short poem by Alexander Pushkin titled "The Cloud" (1835).
2. whist: A trick-taking card game played by four players. It was popular in the eighteenth and nineteenth centuries.
3. *fichu:* A triangular scarf worn around the neck.
4. *à la moujik:* This means "in the peasant style."
5. *"Mon cher, je haïs les hommes pour ne pas mépriser, car autrement la vie serait une farce trop dégoutante":* "My dear friend, I hate men in order not to despise them, otherwise life would be a most repulsive farce." (French)
6. *"Mon cher, je méprise les femmes pour ne pas les aimer, car autrement la vie serait un mélodrame trop ridicule":* "My dear friend, I despise women in order not to love them, otherwise life would be a most ridiculous melodrama." (French)

7. *cherkeska:* A Circassian tunic, worn over the *beshmet.*
8. Beshtau, Zmeinoi, Zheleznaya, and Lisaya: The translation, from Turkish and Russian, of these names: Five-mountains, The Snake, The Iron One, The Bare One.
9. *"Mon dieu, un Circassien!":* "My God, a Circassian!" (French)
10. *"Ne craignez rien, madame—je ne suis pas plus dangereux que votre cavalier.":* "Fear not, madam—I am no more danger-ous than your cavalier." (French)
11. Nogay wagon: The Nogays are an East Caucasian people.
12. *C'est impayable!:* "That's priceless!" (French)
13. This is a reference to Pyotr Pavlovich Kaverin, a friend of Pushkin's who served in the same regiment as Lermontov, and who is mentioned in the first chapter of *Eugene Onegin.*
14. Library for Reading: A journal of the 1830s and 1840s (Biblio-teka dlya Chteniya), which published memoirs and foreign novels, among other things.
15. souls: Serfs in Russia were counted as "souls."
16. From act 3, scene 3 of *Woe from Wit* by Aleksandr Griboedov. It is slightly misquoted by Lermontov here.
17. The cold observations . . . : A fragment from *Eugene Onegin* by Alexander Pushkin.
18. vampire: The vampire referred to here is the hero of a story by John Polidori called "The Vampyre," about a young man who negotiates society by wreaking havoc on the virtuous and en-couraging the sinister.
19. *son coeur et sa fortune:* His heart and his fortune. (French)
20. *arkhaluk:* A Caucasian coat.
21. *"É finita la commedia!":* "The comedy is finished!" (Italian)

3. THE FATALIST

1. *stanitsa:* A large Cossack village.
2. Boston: A card game.
3. faro: A card game that was popular in the eighteenth and nine-teenth centuries, involving an entire pack of playing cards and any number of players.
4. stuss: A variant of the card game faro.
5. *chikhir:* A young red wine from the Caucasus.
6. *uryadnik:* This is a Cossack NCO, a noncommissioned officer.